OUR
ROMANTIC
GETAWAY

OUR
ROMANTIC
GETAWAY

TERI SCHURE

ISBN: 978-1-7352214-0-3 (paperback), 978-1-7352214-1-0 (epub)

Library of Congress Control Number: 2020910792

Printed in the United States of America

10 9 8 7 6 5 4 3 2 1

THIS BOOK   IS DEDICATED
TO MY EVER GROWING   FAMILY.
WE ARE NOT JUST DEFINED BY BLOOD.
IT'S MORE ABOUT WHO STOOD BESIDE
ME, WHO STOOD UP FOR ME, AND
WHO BELIEVED IN ME. AND TO
MY LOVING GRANDMOTHER
MAMMY, WHO REASSURED
ME THAT DUCKS MIGHT
ACTUALLY BE
SWANS.
♡

Well-behaved women seldom make history.

—Laurel Thatcher Ulrich

INTRODUCTION

MY HUSBAND AND I WERE IN DESPERATE NEED OF A vacation. Our lives were becoming less passionate and more stagnant by the day. Our three kids were getting older, going out until all hours, and having the time of their lives. Us? Not so much. I was getting home from my advertising job at eight or nine most nights. Joe, a psychologist, worked at our local high school during the day, had a demanding private practice at night, and was getting home around ten. I would be asleep by the time Joe had dinner and came to bed. As I drifted off to the eleven o'clock news, Joe would be in the kitchen winding down.

Every weekday was the same old routine. And the weekends? We would order takeout on Friday night, so we could eat with the kids, then try to squeeze in some quality family time. Except that the kids always had their own plans, so we would end up eating by ourselves while straining to make small talk. BOR-ing!

Saturday night was "date night." We would go to a restaurant, endure stilted chitchat, come home, catch a movie on Netflix, and then, if the sun, the moon, and the stars aligned, we would have sex. Most of the time, we would pass out on opposite sides of the couch. More boring. And while my relationship with Joe was close, we needed a jump-start. Badly.

Desperate times called for desperate measures. So, I insisted on a romantic getaway. Maybe it was more like persistent pleading. It had been years since the two of us had been able to get away alone. All of our recent vacations had been spent with our kids and almost always involved the two of us prowling around like stalkers, making sure they stayed out of trouble. Not even close to restful or romantic.

Anyway, Joe begrudgingly agreed with my "romantic getaway" idea, although frugal as always, he reminded me how expensive it would be. But we nonetheless booked a seven-day trip to Waves resort in Mexico, sucked up the expense, and went about our ridiculously predictable regimen.

Speaking for myself (Joe was still grumbling about the cost), I was counting down the days until we could chill out and spend some relaxing, romantic alone time together. In between packing and working, I made sure to buy a journal to document the excursion.

As lame as it sounds, ever since I was a kid, I've kept a diary or journal of some kind. I have them all lined up on a bookshelf, labeled by vacations, births, family reunions, and other momentous occasions. This trip would be no exception.

DAY 1

OUR VACATION WAS ABOUT TO BEGIN! AS I STOOD AT the dresser drying my stick-straight brown hair, I discovered Joe's "to-do" list: *Up at 6. Coffee 6:15. Bathroom 6:30. Shower 6:50. Leave money for kids. Weigh suitcase. Cab pickup 7:15. Airport arrival 8:15.*

Even for OCD Joe, this list was a bit much, so I took the liberty of crumpling and throwing it away. Poor Joe. Now he wouldn't know what time to pee. I was determined to make this vacation all about forgetting our routine.

I studied myself in the mirror and was thankful that at forty-two, I could still manage to turn a few heads. At 5'6" and 125 pounds, I was in decent shape and felt good about myself and my accomplishments. But Joe was the star of our family, with his perfect pearly white teeth, thick, wavy light brown hair, and dreamy sky-blue eyes. We have a joke in our family that he is my "McDreamy."

Nothing negative to say about Joe except that he can be overly compulsive and annoyingly frugal.

As I zipped up my suitcase, Joe was running around like a lunatic. "Have you seen my list, Julie? Julie? Julie? Where the hell is my list?"

When we arrived at the airport, the check-in agent informed us that our flight was delayed for two hours. Super annoyed, we sat down at our gate for the long wait. While Joe read *The Economist*, I struck up a conversation with the couple sitting next to me. As we got to know each other better, Celine and Sam told us they were going to The Palm, a resort owned by Inclusive Clubs—the same company that owned Waves.

When the two-hour flight delay became three hours, we all decided to find a bar. After a couple of bloody marys, we were sharing stories and connecting like we had known each other for years. Celine and Sam were both equally attractive, and I was bowled over at how friendly they were. She was a stay-at-home mom, carefree, and vivacious. He was a policeman, lighthearted and hysterically funny. And even though they also had three kids, they somehow found the time and money to go to The Palm every year. I gave Joe a *How come they can go on a yearly vacation and not us?* look. He raised his shoulders in indifference.

Once we boarded the plane, we exchanged seats with another couple so we could sit next to Celine and Sam. Even though we had just met, we wound up gabbing with them the entire flight. By the time we landed, we were like old pals. We picked up our luggage at baggage claim together, and then went over to the Inclusive Clubs check-in area. We were bound for separate resorts and, therefore, different buses, so we said our goodbyes, gave each other hugs and exchanged phone numbers and email addresses.

Joe and I strode over to the Waves desk to arrange for our bus. The lady at the counter checked our reservation on her computer. First, she furiously clicked around the keyboard while studying the screen and then asked us to wait a moment. She proceeded to the other end of the counter and whispered to a man with a nametag that said *Manager* on it.

Joe and I were exasperated. More travel trouble? The plane delay wasn't enough? I was more than ready to get this vacation started.

Mr. Manager and the counter lady huddled up for several minutes, casting nervous glances at us every so often. "This doesn't look good," Joe said as the manager made his way over to us.

"It seems that we have a problem, but it's only a minor

one. Waves is overbooked. Not to worry though, we can put you in one of our other hotels—Exotica."

Exotica??!! Wasn't that the sex-fueled Mexican resort we had seen on a television exposé a few months back? The show featured the free-for-all atmosphere, wild parties, polygamous encounters, orgies, and nudie hot tubs! I was incensed by the manager's suggestion. I eyeballed Joe, who I assumed would be as repulsed as me.

Well, you know what they say about "ass-u-me" because beaming Joe didn't appear to be repulsed *at all*. I needed to put an end to this Exotica nonsense ASAP.

I scowled at Joe. "You're kidding me, right? And what do you think the kids and our parents are going to say about us staying at Exotica?"

"Yeah," Joe echoed to the manager. "We would still want our family to think we're at Waves."

WTF? I glared at Joe, outraged. Mr. Manager winked. "No problemo. We'll deliver your messages to your hotel room twice a day from Waves. That's a standard service we provide for many of our Exotica guests."

Oh, there's a problemo jerkoff, I fumed to myself. But Joe was triumphant. "See, it's a standard service they provide," he repeated, nodding and chuckling—until he saw my expression of incredulity and horror. Then he changed it up and implored, "Julie, please, loosen up. Let's give it a try."

"Loosen up my ass," I replied. But then in horror, I heard myself. "Well, not literally up my ass." The manager and Joe both guffawed as I silently simmered.

The words *absolutely not*, were just about ready to spill out of my mouth, but Joe's demeanor was so boyish and exuberant. And his annoying eagerness, with a side of begging, was wearing me down. I hadn't seen him this fired up since his psychologist convention in Des Moines. And the only reason he was so hepped up about Iowa was their killer mac 'n' cheese.

Despite our tight budget, I was the one who had pushed for the vacation because we needed to break out of our uneventful and repetitive routine. The truth was, our lives had become way too monotonous and plain old stale. I hoped that a vacation together would give us the spark we needed to break out of our predictably predictable life and kick it up a notch. But this kind of kick? Not exactly what I had in mind. Des Moines was way more our speed. Or so I thought.

I gaped at Joe, and his blue puppy-dog eyes. His hands were pressed together in prayer, pleading profusely. But I couldn't hear a word. I was in my own world, imagining us hand in hand on a peaceful, quiet beach with beauteous waves crashing around our feet. I was envisioning the two of us swaying to romantic wafting music, moonbeams shining down on us. No floozies in barely-there bikinis, no raunchy parties, no dirty dancing into the wee hours of the morning. Just me and Joe, in our own little romantic world.

In the distance, I sort of heard Joe. "Julie? Julie? Earth to Julie." When I tuned back in, Joe was giving me a mouthful about our choices being slim to none. The bottom line, Exotica was the only Inclusive Clubs hotel with any available rooms. "Julie, pleeeeasssse," Joe groveled. It was his desperation, and the spark in his McDreamy eyes—which I hadn't seen in forever—that pushed me to change my mind. I wanted to McVomit. But against my better judgment, and notwithstanding my staunch Catholic upbringing, I drove out all thoughts of mortal sin and couldn't believe the words that came out of my mouth. "Fine, you win."

As he processed my answer, Joe's expression was irritatingly cute. So, what else could I do but press on, sickening myself? "Under the circumstances, and given our limited choices, as well as your obnoxiously gung-ho desire..." I paused to give him the full effect of my displeasure before continuing. "I'll give it a shot." My romantic getaway was going downhill fast.

Joe gave me a crushing bear hug, as Mr. Manager pointed us toward the Exotica bus. A dark-haired knock-out, wearing a teeny-weeny bikini top and a pair of shorts that gave new meaning to the term *short shorts*, escorted us to the all-too-conspicuous pink and yellow muraled bus. As I was checking out our transportation, Joe was checking out the short shorts—until I gave him an elbow in his side. Miss Shorty Pants served us a drink called Eros, a delicious tequila concoction. I took a couple of badly needed slugs.

As we boarded the bus, we were shocked to see Celine and Sam sitting in the third row, happily chatting away with a couple in front of them. Feeling the need to fortify myself, I threw back the rest of my drink before making my way down the aisle.

As I looked around, I couldn't help but be inwardly appalled at how everyone was boozing, rubbing, and high-fiving each other. When I turned to Joe, I noticed that his mug was lit up like a jack-o'-lantern. I was contemplating bolting out of the bus door when Sam recognized us.

"Yeah, right, Waves!" Sam said teasingly. "We didn't want to tell you that we were going to Exotica either."

I loudly and defensively explained the overbooking to

him, and everybody on the bus got a laugh out of it—present company excluded. One of the couples called us the "newbies."

"New bees, like bumble?" I asked tentatively. My response evoked even more amusement.

"N-e-w-b-i-e-s," Celine spelled out. "You better watch yourselves at Exotica," she continued. "You guys are fresh meat, and there is nothing more challenging than breaking in a couple of newbies."

It was less than fifteen minutes into the trip, and I was being referred to as fresh meat? *Geezus.* I spun my head around to Joe and whined in his ear that we were in way over our heads.

"Have another Eros," he said soothingly, handing me his drink as we settled in for the hour-long ride. While Celine chattered incessantly, I took stock of Joe interacting with Sam and some of the others. In stark contrast with his usually quiet and shy demeanor, he was thoroughly engaged in the dialogue. Joe will tell you himself, that after umpteen years of psychobabble, outside of his practice, he prefers to be a man of few words. But not today. I watched in wonderment as Joe yack yack yacked away with anyone and everyone on the damn bus—make that the damned bus.

I was marveling at Joe's newly acquired upbeat and carefree attitude, while at the same time, admiring his longish but stylish hair and piercing eyes. I had always been a sucker for his magnetism, and he could usually sweet-talk me into anything with his charm and those baby blues. I leaned on Joe's shoulder. *If ever there was a snafu, this was surely it.*

After about an hour, the bus rolled up to a magnificent, lush outdoor lobby. There was a thatched roof tiki bar out front and another eye-catching muchacha giving out more of the delicious, fruity Eros drink. Two had already made me woozy, but I took the third one anyway; I was no doubt going to need it. We walked up to the reception desk, where another Mexican stunner greeted us. *Was there no end to the white teeth, big boobs, and cutie patooties?* I discreetly checked myself out in the mosaic mirror behind the front desk.

The drop-dead gorgeous girl addressed Joe. "We want to apologize for the overbooking. And because of the inconvenience we've caused you, you're being upgraded to a deluxe ocean-view theme room."

"Theme room?" I mentally prepared myself for her answer.

"You'll see," she said coquettishly. I was reasonably

sure that I did not want to see. Then she followed up with, "Do you prefer the nude side or the prude side?"

NUDE SIDE? There's a nude side to this place?? No way was I staying on the nude side of anything. "Prude side," I proclaimed definitively, just as Joe was simultaneously chirping "nude side." I gave him a heated glare while the gorgeous one explained to us that clothes were optional on the prude side. *Optional?*

"Our option is to stay on the prude side," I answered firmly, giving Joe my infamous evil eye. Charm or no charm, enough was enough.

Joe backed down immediately. "Agreed. We want to stay on the prude side. The nude side thing was a joke." He gave me his meathead smile. "Such a kidder," I quipped back at him. I gave him a killer smile back and gently caressed his arm—*you lying sack of shit.*

Just at that moment, a nude couple strode into the lobby and approached the counter right next to us. I almost fainted right then and there. Joe's eyeballs were just about bulging out of his head. The man had a gold ring around his penis, and the woman had electric blue hair "down there." As I gazed at Joe, horrified, he was giving the couple a neighborly "hello." *HELLO?*

Then Joe turned to me with a broad shit-eating

grin—until he saw my squinting, you-better-straighten-up-in-a-hurry mean-girl eyes. Not knowing where to look at that point, he snatched the activity brochure sitting on the counter and proceeded to read it to me.

"Every night has a different theme, Julie!" I gave Joe a blank stare as he waved the handout in my face. "And tonight is Skimpy Bathing Suit Night at the disco!"

Joe, please, calm yourself. I tried not to check out the asses of Miss Blue Hair and her penis ring guy as they sauntered away. Like in this lifetime, I would ever wear a bathing suit to go dancing, let alone a so-called "skimpy suit." To be clear, I rarely wear a bathing suit at all.

Joe pointed excitedly to the brochure. "Oh, Julie, we need to go disco dancing tonight." *Need* to go disco dancing? Joe doesn't even dance. The last time I danced with Joe was at our wedding—and I had to twist his arm. When I reminded him that he doesn't dance, he gave me his friggin baby blues and said, "We're on vacation, remember?" Sure, now that a skimpy something was involved, he was all for getting his dancing shoes on. And anyway, didn't disco die out like thirty years ago?

"I'll call for a bellhop to take you to your room," said the desk goddess. "Oh, and we have just one rule around here." *Oh, just one?* Based on what I had seen so far, this rule was sure to be a beaut. "No cameras allowed anywhere on the premises," she said empathetically, pointing her finger in my direction. *Oh, don't you worry, miss lady behind the desk; there isn't a chance in hell I will ever produce a single shred of photographic evidence of our stay here.*

An athletic young man approached us and took us to our room. He had the kind of face that stopped you in your tracks. *Were there no ugly or overweight people in this joint?* I self-consciously sucked in my stomach.

The buff bellhop opened the double doors to reveal a lavish room in Roman decor, with massive columns and mirrors. "Welcome to Caesar's Court."

The king-size bed was on a platform and surrounded by stone statues and Roman columns. The marble tub was the size of a small pool and overlooked the ocean. Next to the hot tub was an elaborate marble urn draped with red and green grapes, cheese, fruit, and a bottle of expensive champagne.

I took in the sensational decor, and okay, I was impressed—until a glimmer on the ceiling caught my attention. Directly above the bed was an ostentatious gold bedazzled mirror with pulleys in each corner, with hooks and ropes attached to them. For me, total buzzkill. For Joe, absolute nirvana as he gazed hypnotically upward.

Apparently, the room decor and accouterments were not killing *his* buzz.

When the stud muffin bellboy saw me scrutinizing the setup, he casually said, "Use of the apparati is up to one's discretion." *There's a plural for apparatus?* As Joe dreamily gaped up at the machinery, I sped across the room, as far away from the bed as possible. Clothes were optional, apparati was discretionary. *What the hell?*

I was already tipsy from the three drinks I had consumed, so I told Joe to keep the champagne on ice, and we would come back to the room and drink it later.

As I shoved some cheese and fruit into my mouth, I purposefully and deliberately avoided looking up at the ceiling. Then I unpacked my suitcase, put on my not-even-close-to-skimpy bathing suit, grabbed my sunglasses and suntan lotion, and headed off to the beach with Joe.

As we took the path to the ocean, we came to a fork in the sand where there were two signs in the shape of arrows. One sign pointed to the "Prude Beach" and the other to the "Nude Beach." Without breaking stride, Joe made a sharp right toward the nude beach. But as he turned, he peered over his shoulder and saw me glowering. He instantaneously pivoted and marched in step behind me to the prude beach.

After another twenty yards or so, through a majestic palm tree grove, we emerged at a sparkly white beach with sand that squeaked as our feet sunk into it. The water was as blue and clear as a cloudless sky. But to my astonishment, the prude beach was completely deserted! There were rows and rows of empty chairs and not a soul to be found.

"People are probably still checking in," Joe answered in response to my quizzical expression as he pulled up two lounge chairs. We sat peacefully, holding hands and taking in the magnificent ocean view, while Mexican music wafted through the air. *Exotica might not be so bad*, I thought.

Apparently, I thought way too soon because a few minutes later, I focused my attention on what seemed to be roaring and cheering in the distance. Where was the noise coming from? Joe was stretching his neck to see what was transpiring as I lathered zinc oxide on my nose. There was a dense expanse of palm trees blocking our view, so Joe made his way to the edge of the water to get a better look.

"You are NOT going to believe what's going on," he said after sprinting back to our chairs. At this point, I was ready to believe anything. "The nude side of the beach is packed. It's like the Hamptons on a holiday weekend."

Pssh, like this den of iniquity resembles anything remotely close to the Hamptons.

He gazed at me with his twinkling, starting-to-really-annoy-me eyes. "I'm not going. Case closed." We both sat mutely, trying to ignore the singing, clapping, and chanting coming from the nude beach.

Despite the clamoring, I shut my eyes and must have dozed off. When I woke up, Joe's beach chair was empty. Well, empty except for his bathing suit trunks. I bolted out of my chair, whipping my head from side to side. *Where the hell was Joe?*

There he was, about two hundred yards away, a towel wrapped around his waist, facing the nude brouhaha. I blared out his name and stormed over to him. "What part of 'I'm not going over there' didn't you understand?"

When he turned around, his usually bright eyes were dull and glazed over. "Then I'm going there without you. I'll bring you back a report."

I placed my hands on my hips. "You're not going anywhere without me."

"Then take off your bathing suit and let's go. Otherwise, I *am* going without you."

I was trying to back down from the argument gracefully. I didn't want to give in, but what choice did I have? "If I go, I go with my suit on."

He headed toward the ruckus in a semi-trance.

"Do what you want. But, please wipe the zinc oxide off your nose."

As we got closer to the nude beach, the scene was frightfully unforgettable. At the ocean side of the beach, there was a group of stark-naked partiers under a banner that read "Bubbly Doubles." As we got closer, a few people from the group approached us. We explained what had happened with the overbooking, and they introduced us around, reiterating our story. Someone mentioned that there was another couple bumped from Waves, and they promised to bring them over to meet us.

The "Bubbles," as they called themselves, were having a contest to see how many bottles of champagne they could open and consume in a two-hour period. They were meticulously keeping track on an accounting ledger pad and passing around the champagne—and excellent champagne at that—to the entire nude side of the beach.

We passed a blonde sex kitten with breasts the size of cantaloupes. The only thing she had on was a gold belly chain with a diamond thunderbolt pointing toward her vajayjay. Not wanting to stare, I nonchalantly took my sunglasses off the top of my head and put them on. No way was I going to let anyone catch me checking out their private parts.

Cantaloupe Breasts proceeded to bend over to fish out a bottle of champagne from the cooler. Her ass was literally in our faces. I quickly averted my eyes. But not Joe. He was too engrossed in her ass to avert anything. When she got up and handed Joe a bottle of champagne, his eyes shifted from her ass to her breasts, and he was so flipping preoccupied, he almost dropped the bottle. I gave him a sharp jab and focused my attention on the surrealistic scene in front of us. It was imminently clear that the only way I was going to make it through this shitstorm of a vacation was by drinking a river of booze. I snatched the champagne bottle from Joe and took a swig.

We took a path up from the beach toward the nude-side pool to take a peek. NOT a good idea. The pool was standing room only, flanked on both sides with two enormous hot tubs that were swarming with naked-on-naked guests. The goings-on in the pool and tubs were like nothing I had ever seen before, and they made the Exotica television exposé seem G-rated. Glistening men and women were draped all over each other, while others were twisted together like pretzels. There was a puppy pile of bodies contorted in positions I didn't know was feasibly possible. These were some very limber folks.

Men were fondling two and three women at a time,

and one particularly well-endowed blonde Adonis was sandwiched between two spellbinding female deities. Upon closer observation, I realized that the two women had penises. Whoa. *I could use a Disney movie right about now.* I took another chug out of the bottle of champagne.

Periodically, the partners switched, and it was impossible to figure out who belonged to whom. Joe gave me his megawatt smile and said, "Toto, I have a feeling we're not in Kansas anymore." *Not even Toto would be safe in this place*, I warned myself.

Almost all of the women, and many of the men, had little to no pubic hair. And for the few who did, it was every color in the rainbow. I marveled at the living and breathing interactive color wheel options.

As I witnessed the drunken debauchery taking place around me, I felt like a bit player smack in the middle of a porno film. I took another swig of champagne as Miss Cantaloupe Breasts strolled over and introduced us to a straight-out-of-Hollywood-looking duo. "Here's the other couple who got bumped from Waves."

I gave Kendra and Don the once-over, and couldn't help but notice that they were dead ringers for the Barbie and Ken dolls. She was a leggy bombshell of a blonde with flawless skin and perfect bone structure, and he was toned, tan, and gorgeously rugged. "Can you believe our luck at getting bumped?" Don asked, beaming. When he noticed me scowling, he just shook his head. Then Kendra chimed in. "Well, as they say in boating ALL ABOARD!." *All aboard? Sorry, Barbie, but the only boat that comes to my mind is the Titanic.*

Don led us to a table *in* the mammoth wave pool; its rippling water surged around our feet as if we were wading into the ocean. The bar was in the center of the pool, surrounded by tables. The stools were submerged in the water, and like the sea, the pool got deeper as you walked further into it. Directly above us was an upper bridge and deck lined with cabanas.

We all looked up in fascination as a dripping wet drunk dude ran from cabana to cabana spilling his drink all over everyone. His last run was hard to watch and must have been incredibly painful. As he sprinted to a crowded cabana, he put on the brakes with his bare feet and was literally airborne—a good two feet into the air. Parallel to the deck floor, he landed smack into the middle of his circle of friends. Despite the noise of the ooooh's and gasps around me, I could hear the dull, loud THUD. He was lucky that he landed on his side and sort of slid across the deck. The four of us tried to control ourselves, but the hilarity of the deck scene got the better of us, and we lost it.

At the opposite end of the pool, was a thunderous waterfall, which cascaded down onto a sprawling mass of entwined body parts.

To the left and right of the pool were the two hot tubs, overflowing with trim and slim revelers. I had never seen so many naked and in-shape people in one place in my entire life. Come to think of it; I had never seen so many naked people, period.

Still wearing my bathing suit, I was mentally egging my prissy self on, while simultaneously shutting my prissy self down. *Should I get nude? Nah, I'm good.* I hugged my arms tightly around my chest.

I took a break from my conflicted state and eyed the wacky scene. Women were dancing on the tables in the water, and tanning oil was being rubbed here there and everywhere. Men on men, men on women, women on women—I was rattled. There were wall-to-wall bodies everywhere—posing, flirting, locking lips, grinding on each other, and sporting enough silicone and saline implants to fill an Olympic-size pool. *Who knew I needed a penicillin shot for this trip?*

The pool was standing room only as we stood waist deep, analyzing the scene. I was still wearing my bathing suit, Don and Joe were nude, and Kendra was topless with her snow-white ass hanging out of her thong bottom. *Thank God for my sunglasses.*

As I chatted with Kendra, a male security guard in an impressive uniform walked over to me. "Ma'am, you're breaking the rules. You're on the nude side of Exotica, so at the very least, you'll need to remove your bathing suit top."

My first thought was, *Who the F is this guy, the clothes police?* And then I remembered where I was. *Duh, yeah!* "Let's go back to our chairs on the prude beach," I pleaded to Joe. "Oh, come on; it's just your top," Kendra said.

"She's a nude prude, y'all," said a woman doggy paddling next to us. Joe, Kendra, and Don found the remark humorous. I quietly fumed. She introduced herself as Baryl and her husband as David. Baryl was a classic blonde who could have graced any magazine cover. She had flowing golden curls and an endearing thick southern drawl. To prove I wasn't that much of a prude, I gave the security guard a defiant glare, pulled off my top, twirled it around my finger, and wrapped it around Joe's neck.

Suddenly I realized that we had an audience, as a group of guests around us cheered and clapped. Joe clapped the hardest until I gave him a death stare.

I was feeling uncomfortably exposed, squeamish, and

uneasy. Yet I had to admit, it also felt slightly liberating. I was sure it was the champagne and Eros cocktails that had me feeling so fearless, but whatever the reason, I was getting gutsier by the minute. I was also getting drunker by the minute.

"So, Kendra," I said, trying to block out the lunacy. "Now that you're here, do you think you'll do anything misguided?"

She raised her eyebrows at me for a second. "Guided in what way?" *I get it. Three syllables. It's a lot.* I mentally tried to drum up a more straightforward, two-syllable word. "You know, like ill-advised?" Kendra stared vacuously back at me and then asked me to speak to her in English. *How about stupid, does stupid register?*

I threw out the word loose, and she seemed to get that. "I guess it would depend on your definition of loose, but who knows? If I had a partner in crime, I might get loose."

Partner in crime? Believe me, the goings-on around here was surely a crime. As I took in the ghastly festivities, the only thing on my mind was how much I wanted to take a shower. Make that a cold shower. And from what I could see of Joe's not so little willy—he needed a cold shower as well.

I was way past lightheaded, and I had consumed too many drinks in too short a time. I wanted to go back to the room, but it was no surprise to me that Joe wanted to stay.

I thought about leaving Joe there, because I needed to lie down—before I fell down. A song by Seal was playing, and as the words, "We're never gonna survive unless we get a little crazy," wafted across the pool, I glanced over at Joe. He was moving to the music and staring up at a well-endowed brunette, glistening with sweat, sensually running her hands down her perfect naked form on the bridge staring back at him. *No chance was I leaving Joe here without me.* So, I dragged him back to the beach chairs on the prude side to pick up our stuff and back to our room.

Before we left, we made plans with Kendra, Don, Baryl, and David to meet at the "Group Therapy" bar at eight o'clock for a drink at cocktail hour before dinner. Just what I needed—more drinks. And Joe, ever the psychologist, was droning on incessantly about the name of the bar like it was our destiny. By the end of this trip, I was, without question, going to need some serious therapy. Make that couples therapy.

I did have to admit, though, that it was remarkably easy getting to know people here. It would usually take us months or even years to find one couple, let alone two, to go out to dinner with, but here we had been able to make four friends in less than an hour.

When we got back to the room, Joe and I had the best sex we'd had in at least ten years. Then Joe passed out. I was exhausted but couldn't sleep. I was majorly wigged out by the whole bizarre "lay of the land" and couldn't stop speculating about what might happen next.

Be careful what you wish for, I thought to myself, recalling how much I wanted this vacation. *This may turn out to be the longest week of your life.*

Joe woke up at seven-thirty and made a mad dash for the shower. I was already dressed and had popped the champagne. And even though I promised myself not to, I couldn't help but look up at the mirror on the ceiling. After an afternoon of the bold and beautiful, my insecurities were creeping into my psyche. My mousy brown hair drooped around my pale cheeks. I hated that my hair had no hint of a curl or wave, but at least it worked for the heat and humidity of Mexico. I had always kept in shape, jogging, weight training, and watching my diet, but I was no match for some of these women. And okay, the grueling stomach exercises I forced myself to do every day for weeks before this trip, had thankfully paid off. But I was feeling ordinary and unsure of myself.

If the nude pool was any indication of what attire to expect at dinner, my just-above-the-knee yellow dress was going to be white bread conservative. I sized up my front and backside and decided to lose the bra. My breasts were showing through my dress, and I started to second guess myself. But then I figured if I could go topless at the pool, no harm done with a little tata reveal. As I gave myself the green light, I thought about what my mother would say about all of this, or worse, the kids! I shuddered and put all thoughts of family out of my champagne-and-Eros-blurred mind.

Joe came out of the bathroom and did a double-take. When his eyes shifted up from my chest, I was shocked that they were filled with tears. Joe was teary over the fact that I was braless? He pulled me into his arms and cradled me adoringly. *Way out of character for Joe, but who was I to complain?* Joe kissed me passionately, wanting to get down to it again. "Sorry, Joe, nobody messes with my cocktail hour." Joe had to agree because he knows I'm a sucker for anything that has to do with hors d'oeuvres. When it comes to any function or event that entails a cocktail hour, I insist on being there on time, so I can stuff myself silly.

He gently caressed my face with his hands. As he

kissed me lightly on my neck, my body was tingling all over. Even though I was still having significant issues with the whole Exotica experience, it was uncovering passions I hadn't felt in forever.

On our way to the restaurant, we passed a slew of risqué, undeniably attractive men and women strutting around in outrageous, yet bewitching outfits. Women were wearing micro-mini glitter dresses, leather outfits that covered just about nothing, latex getups, boy shorts, skimpy bathing suits, and everything and anything else imaginable. Not that I could have ever imagined the scene before me.

The scantily clad women pranced around in shoes that gave new meaning to *high heels*. I was lucky if I could handle two-inchers. Most of these women were wearing four and five-inch heels. They were more like stilts. And I had to agree with Joe that they made their legs appear incredibly long and sexy. *Wait a sec; now I was commiserating with Joe about how sexy these women were?*

I confided to Joe that compared to these women, I felt like I was wearing a burka. He started to kid around, picturing me parading around Exotica covered from head to toe in a black cloak, with net screening over the slits for my eyes. Joe pulled me close. "This is insane, Julie; I feel like a teenager again. Thank you for doing this with me." I ruffled his hair, overjoyed that he said thanks for doing this *with* me, instead of thanks for doing this *for* me. *Hmm…maybe overjoyed was pushing it.*

When we got to the Group Therapy bar, I asked Joe to order me a glass of champagne. "I hope you'll be able to handle yourself after all this alcohol, Julie." *Telegram for Joe! Julie won't be able to handle herself without all this alcohol.*

The bar was packed with more over-the-top hotties and hunks. Behind the bar was a human aquarium, where several topless women undulated in mermaid tails. As I followed their movements in fascination, a couple approached us and introduced themselves.

At home, if a strange couple ever came up to us to start a conversation, we'd think that was weird. But people were so outgoing here, and they genuinely wanted to reach out and get to know us. Then I remembered the *newbie* thing and wondered if all the friends we were making had an ulterior motive. I was finally enjoying myself, so I tried not to get too hung up on the reasons for their friendliness.

But as the crowd got rowdier and touchier, I envisioned myself turning into "fresh meat," and hastily made my way over to an infinity pool next to the bar. In the water were several pool tables, and there was a topless, sultry and busty platinum blonde in a microscopic bikini bottom, lying on one of them. Her bangs obscured the top half of her face like a sheepdog.

Men, as well as women, were taking turns pouring liquor in her belly button and licking it off of her. Joe interrupted my burning stare. "Body shots." I frowned at him, displeased. As if reading my mind, he added, "Not that I ever did one."

Just then, Celine and Sam showed up. Celine wrapped her arms around me like we had been friends forever. My friends back home would never hold me like that. The people we were meeting at Exotica were so eager to be our "besties," and I was beginning to feel surprisingly comfortable with them. *Don't get too comfortable, girlfriend.*

Kendra, Don, Baryl, and David found us at the bar, and the eight of us made our way to a table for dinner. Celine and Sam caught my attention for the first time. Sam's handsome face was chiseled, and he had a playful smile. Celine was wearing a tiny bikini top and boy shorts that made her long shapely legs look like they had no end. And I hadn't noticed her voluptuous, baseball-shaped breast implants before.

When we first met at the airport, I thought Celine was

pretty, but in a plain-Jane way. But she was far from plain tonight. As she sashayed in front of me, I couldn't help but admire her butt cheeks peeping out from under her shorts. Her long lustrous dark hair was in stark contrast to her pale and almost naked body. *I'm losing it, right?*

The dining room at first glance was seemingly ordinary; until I focused on the waitresses serving drinks in micro-bikinis combined with the severely underdressed patrons milling about. And I don't mean underdressed as in blue jeans. An overly-bleached blonde woman meandered past our table wearing nothing but a necklace. That was it—one single strand of pearls. Joe was ogling her, while I shifted around anxiously, hoping there wasn't anything communicable on my chair.

During dinner, we all took turns trading stories about our lives, our routines, and our experiences. But this was not your ordinary Saturday-night-out dinner conversation with friends. Laced in with all the talk were intimate and sexual details about each of the couples' private lives. Everyone was open to discussing topics we would never dream of bringing up back home. And the more each couple shared about their innermost thoughts and secrets, the more others opened up about theirs.

It might possibly have been the deepest and most honest discourse we'd ever had with other couples. We were all revealing stuff that I would never dare to divulge to anyone but Joe. And the sexual undertone was undeniable.

Celine and Sam told us they were swingers. In their words, they liked to hook up with other couples. "Aren't you afraid it will screw up your marriage?" I asked, bewildered that they thought having sex with anyone but each other was okay.

"Since we started swapping, our marriage has never been better," said Celine.

"Well, I could never be with another man," I said adamantly.

"You don't have to," said Sam. "Whatever turns you on. That's what it's all about. You know, do your own thing."

"Yeah, whatever y'all ah comfortable with," said Baryl in that drawl of hers, while David nodded in agreement.

Joe was nodding in agreement, too, until I gave him a dirty look. *Whatever y'all are comfortable with? I wasn't even comfortable talking about it!*

Kendra and Don were next. Don used to be a professional hockey player in Canada and was coaching a college team in Buffalo. Kendra was a former model and now the mother of two girls, as well as a gym teacher at their local high school. They had been to Waves a couple of times, and once they had even taken a tour of Exotica. So, when they got bumped from Waves, they knew what to expect.

Baryl and David were "soft swap swingers" from Kentucky. "Soft swap?" I asked, baffled. David explained that Baryl was into girls, but that the guys get involved "peripherally." "Peripherally?" I asked cautiously, not sure I wanted to know what that meant.

"Ah love girls," Baryl said blissfully, ignoring my question. "How 'bout you, darlin'? Y'all ever have a fee-male experience?"

"Never," I responded overly-adamantly. I felt myself blush, because, OKAY, I had thought about doing it with a girl in college, but then I di'int!

To my relief, the subject was dropped, and everyone was busy chatting it up and getting to know each other. I was sitting quietly, feeling slightly woozy, and ruminating over the precise definition of "peripherally." Baryl was practically sitting on my lap and was gently touching and stroking my arm as she spoke. She brushed her fingers lightly up and down my back. "You are so dang purty. Ah was proud of you takin' yer bathin' suit top off raht there in the pool," she continued in her cute drawl, while her hand moved from my back to my left leg. *Trouble!*

Her hand felt incredibly soft and warm—so different from Joe's masculine hands. She also smelled delicious, and it hit me that I was enjoying Baryl's company just a tad too much. I scanned around the table to see if anyone was on to us, but they were all caught up in their own discussions.

To be honest, at this point, I could barely hear a thing, since I was a wary but apparently willing participant in our tryst. Baryl whispered in my ear, skillfully breathing into the inner part of it and making my body shiver. "Are yer breasts real, darlin'?" she asked softly, still breathing hot air into my ear. I gave her a down-and-up movement with my head. I couldn't even get words out at that point. I had the goosies all over my body as her soft hand went higher up my dress. *First intoxicating, and now the goosies?!* I wanted to stop Baryl, but the feeling was like nothing I had ever experienced—so I let her fingers do the walking.

I was becoming more "worked up" by the second, and was terrified about what might happen next. But I didn't stop Baryl's roving hand. I was overcome by a swell of intense pleasure. With my eyes closed, I felt sure I was going to explode any second, until Baryl demurely purred, "Lemmie know when y'all are ready for the real thang." Then she abruptly took her hand off my leg and made off with Sam to the dance floor.

I felt like cold water had just been dumped all over me, and I finally came to my senses. I was appalled and mortified that she had gotten me to that "place," and was praying that no one had been watching. But everyone was blathering away and hadn't noticed me at all.

I side-peeked at Baryl as inconspicuously as possible. The thought of having "the real thang" with Baryl was at once both repulsive and intriguing. Baryl leered back at me wickedly and slithered her hands down her body. *Can somebody please slap me back to reality?*

Awakened from my stupor, I slowly turned from Baryl to Joe, who was deeply engrossed in a tête-à-tête with Kendra. As it happened, their têtes were way too close for my comfort.

Joe was openly flirting, and when Kendra put her hand on his leg, I just about had a meltdown. "Let's dance," I snapped at Joe as I yanked him to the dance floor.

Baryl came over to us and whispered in my ear again, this time asking me if I was going to the disco later. *Just nod and agree, and hopefully, she'll go away.* She perceived my nod to be an assent. "Y'all save me a dance now, ya hear?"

As Baryl left the dance floor, I again began to fantasize about her and then shook my head clear. I needed to get out of there pronto, so I told Joe I wanted to go to the room to fool around before going to the disco. Joe was more than happy to oblige.

After more phenomenal sex, followed by a much-needed nap, I was ready to stay in bed for the rest of the night. But Joe had "disco on the brain," so I reluctantly agreed. Since the theme for the night was skimpy bathing suits, Joe wanted me to model some of mine for him. And even though I had earlier sworn off wearing a bathing suit to the disco, I bravely strutted around in my bikini, twirling around the Greek statues like I was Cleopatra. *And we all know what happened to her.*

Given the next-to-nothing dinner outfits everyone was wearing, Joe wasn't convinced that any of the bathing suits I tried on were skimpy enough for the disco. As much as I didn't want to agree with him, I realized he was right. And in my newly perverted (and inebriated) way of seeing things, I not only wanted to look sexy for Joe, but I also had Baryl on the brain. *So, sue me.*

In any event, I chose the "skimpiest" bikini I could find. Even though it was relatively tame, I still felt uncomfortable gallivanting around with just a bathing suit, so I threw on a wrap to wear as a skirt.

I mentioned to Joe that maybe we could buy something a little sexier at the boutique the next day. *Wait, now I needed sexier clothing?* Joe's face morphed into the Cheshire Cat. "Absolutely. My wallet is open for you." *Joe's wallet is open for me, yay??* I never thought I would hear my all-too-thrifty husband say that!

Joe, in his new Cheshire Cat guise, purred at me. "Julie, you look hot, hot, hot." *Here we go again!* After completing a record third round of sex in one day, we showered and then ran off to the disco. Well, Joe ran while I reluctantly followed.

The disco was packed, and the mood super-charged. And yes, there was a mirrored disco ball smack in the middle of the most bizarre disco ever. People were rubbing against each other, dirty dancing, making out, and everything was pretty much no holds barred—literally and figuratively. Ladies intertwined themselves with other ladies, and couples were oscillating suggestively, with two women in the middle and a man at each end. And then there were five or six women lined up, one behind the other, grinding together in some sick X-rated version of a conga line.

Right behind the conga free-for-all, I caught a glimpse of David dance-humping Baryl. I didn't even know that was a thing. The buzz I was feeling from a full day of alcohol and sun was turning into a major migraine, and the full impact of the Exotica decision was starting to sink in. What better time for another Eros?!

What I should do is to scoot my skimpy-bathing-suit ass to the front desk and demand a new hotel or the first plane out of here, I thought as Joe came back with my drink. He thankfully sensed my anxiety and turned a blind eye as I gulped my Eros.

The tequila drinks were going down way too easy. And fast. When I caught Joe gawking at two girls making out, I pinched his arm hard. He grabbed my hand and pulled me onto the dance floor. This new found Joe dragging me to dance was yet another warning sign that I needed to keep my eye on him. Make that both eyes.

There were two girls gyrating on a pole on the stage by the dance floor. They moved like pros, but I recognized them as guests from our time at the pool that afternoon. The crowd was admiring them and cheering them on. The brunette was wearing a tiny leopard thong and had a tattoo on her back of two Asian-shaped blue eyes. Her tattooed eyes were so captivating that I couldn't stop staring at them. Perhaps it was because of the gazillion drinks I had consumed, but I could swear the eyes were staring back at me. *Sure, Julie, have another drink.*

The blonde was wearing a floral one-piece thong

bathing suit that was so sheer I could see right through it. As I got closer, I realized that both their outfits were literally painted on them. I was in awe of their perfectly painted bodies. Their unpainted bodies were close to perfect as well. The guy who slid across the deck earlier was screaming, "crank it up, crank it up." Under any other circumstances, I wouldn't have recognized him, but his scabby friction burn was a dead giveaway. *Somebody, please, give this guy a shirt.*

"How revolting!" a pretty but overly distressed red-head blurted out.

"Which part? The pole, the girls, the scabby guy, the disco, or the resort?" I asked her.

"The whole skeevy thing," she responded. With tears in her eyes, she asked me if I wanted to go to the bar for a drink.

I jokingly informed Joe that I was getting a drink with my new, having-a-breakdown friend. He was so enthralled with the two girls on stage that he merely gave me a wave of his hand and said, "Uh-huh." I was sure he didn't have a clue what I told him or where I was going.

"Two Eros," I told the bartender. Then I turned my attention to my new, teary-eyed BFF. "Is it two Eros or two Eroses?" I asked her, which seemed to lighten her mood. "What's your name?" I asked as we clicked our glasses together.

"Mary," she answered, and dabbed the tears off her cheek with a bar napkin imprinted with a cartoon of a nude stripper, pole dancing.

"Are you here with someone?"

"Yes, my husband, Stan," Mary replied, her voice cracking. "We had a nasty fight, and he stormed off. He's a lawyer, so I can never win an argument. He told me to come back to the room when I was ready to discuss Exotica rationally."

Like Exotica and rational belong in the same sentence, I thought as Mary blew her nose all over the stripper girl on the bar napkin.

Although I didn't ask, and didn't really care, Mary proceeded to tell me her life story. She had been married for almost a decade, and the whole time, all Stan ever wanted to do was to take an Exotica vacation. "I've been saying *no* to him for almost ten years. What kind of a girl does he think I am anyway? He would be thrilled if I got up on the stage and danced on the pole like a ho." As tears were flowing down her cheeks, I tried to make her feel better. I told her about the overbooking and how out of my comfort zone I felt. That calmed her down a decibel.

"How about if we go find your husband?" I asked her, starting to wonder where mine was.

"You would go get him with me?" she asked, taken aback.

"Sure, let me go rescue my husband first," I said, nervously scanning the disco for Joe. If there was anyone who needed rescuing, it was me, and it was obvious that Joe wasn't the least bit concerned about it.

When I got to the dance floor, Baryl was sandwiched in between Joe and David, and the three were dirty dancing together! It was more like grinding than dancing, and Mary asked, "Are you sure your husband hasn't done this before? And by the way, which one is your husband? I would kill Stan if he did that."

I had to admit that I did have murderous thoughts as I watched the three of them. How naïve I was to assume it was *me* who Baryl wanted. I yanked Joe, a.k.a. Fred f-ing Astaire, by the arm and gave him my best, you-better-watch-yourself-buddy stare. He obediently followed me to the bar.

"Mellow out," Joe said. "I was just having some fun."

"Too much fun if you ask me," I said icily, then introduced him to Mary.

Mary gave the two of us a hug and thanked me for being so supportive. "You're the best," she said as she kissed me on the cheek.

Once again, I was astonished at how quickly I was meeting and getting close to people at Exotica. It would typically take me years to get close enough to someone to open up like I was to Mary. Even though it felt like high school, I was enjoying it. And evidently, in addition to being Mary's new BFF, I was now going to be Mary's marriage mediator. Just call me Judge Julie.

While Mary went to the bathroom, I gave Joe a short rundown of the situation. He was not interested in playing middleman. "We have to at least escort her back to her room," I told him.

"Okay, but let's make it quick," Joe responded vacantly, too busy drooling over a topless girl sucking on a lollipop to even make eye contact with me.

The three of us left the disco for Mary and Stan's room. This meetup was going to be interesting.

When we got to the room, Mary unlocked the door and told us she would be right out. "You brought a couple back with you?" we heard Stan ask.

"It's not like that," I heard Mary tell Stan. "They don't want to be here either."

Joe scoffed and said, "What exactly did you tell her?"

Before I could answer, Stan came out with Mary. For what reason, I don't know, but I began to blab to Stan about the overbooking, how out of my element I felt, and how I understood Mary's concerns.

"Thanks for sharing," Stan replied dryly, cutting me off. I gave Stan a stink face. "I'm just trying to help you out here." Then Stan backed off. "I get it. My apologies. Look, maybe you can calm Mary down because I certainly haven't been able to. She's ruining our vacation. Just because we're here doesn't mean I want to be with anyone else. I just thought it would be a lot more exciting than the usual vanilla vacations we always take."

To Joe's surprise, and for that matter, mine as well, I told Stan that I *partially* understood where he was coming from. And while I was not interested in participating in any of the goings-on at Exotica, particularly the part about being with someone else's husband, I was warming up to the place. "Should warming up give me hope?" Joe asked, wryly. I was hoping my look daggers answered his wise-ass question.

While the four of us made our way back to the disco, Stan and Mary tried to talk out their differences. "I'm sorry you're upset, but you need to chill out Mary; it's a once-in-a-lifetime experience."

"You got that right," Mary retorted, "because we will *never* be back here again."

"So, then let's at least enjoy ourselves while we *are* here," Stan replied.

Joe and I bobbed our heads in agreement. Then the two of us noticed each other bobbing, and we stopped dead in our tracks. "Get a load of us," I said to Stan. "We're totally in over our heads and agreeing with you like we know anything about anything."

When we got to the disco bar, Kendra and Don flagged us down. "Hey, you guys interested in going to the beachside café for a burger?" Don asked. The late-night scene unfolding around us was getting more outlandish by the minute, so we happily said yes. The six of us hungrily piled our trays with hot dogs, burgers, and fries.

It was now 2 a.m., and I was not only working on my second dinner but also trying to soak up the mass quantities of alcohol in my body. The last time I was up at 2 a.m. was to take care of a screaming baby. As I reassessed the past few hours, I concluded that screaming babies might be preferable.

As we stuffed ourselves, the six of us opened up to each other about our sometimes tedious and always monogamous lives. In the middle of disclosing the details of our relationships, Baryl and David showed up. "They're soft swap swingers," I confided to Mary, who scrunched up her nose. *Now I was the authority on swingers?*

"What's a soft spot?" she asked.

"No, a soft *swap*!" I corrected her. "Anyway, I'll tell you later. And don't worry," I continued in her ear. "It's me she's after."

The sudden look of terror in Mary's eyes cracked both of us up. "Y'all need to let me in on yer little secret," Baryl said sarcastically.

"This is the nude prude table," I jokingly replied. "Are you sure you want to sit with us?"

"As long as y'all ain't catchy," Baryl drawled.

And then, in what seemed like one long psychology session, we all told our separate stories. The entire group loved the fact that Joe was a shrink. Baryl was a teacher, and David was an accountant. Baryl and David had been married for nine years before they decided to test the swinger waters.

It turned out Baryl had been exclusive with girls in high school and college. But then she met David, who was originally from Baltimore, at the end of her senior year, and she "switched teams." "He was the only guy ah have ever bin attracted to," she said. "Ah was raised in a strict

Baptist house, and David was raised Jewish, and ah ended up convertin' to his religion raht before we got engaged," she continued.

"Wow," I said, "your parents must have been upset when you converted."

"Sweety Pah, they was so relieved ah was datin' a man, religion was the last thing they was carin' about." We all got a chuckle out of that.

Then it was David's turn to dish. "We aren't swingers in the true sense, like full swapping with couples or anything close to that. It's just that Baryl likes to hang out with girls from time to time, which is fine with me."

"Yeah, and men get involved 'peripherally,' right?" I said, like a know-it-all big shot.

"What does that mean, and how do you know that?" Mary asked, nervously. David explained that Baryl likes to have sex with women while the men watch and sometimes get involved, but they don't have intercourse with anyone but their spouses.

"So, anything else goes, except for intercourse?" I asked.

"That about sums it up, dahlin," said Baryl, giving me a grossly suggestive wink, which was my cue to exit. I shot out of my chair and interrupted the conversation with, "Who wants a drink?" Looking for a way out of the talkfest, and desperate to escape Baryl's not-so-subtle advances, I took drink requests and trekked over to the bar next to the café.

Everywhere you turned, there was a bar, which was turning out to be one of the few positives about this place. I was going to need plenty of bars to get through the week. *Peripherally, my ass.*

When I got back with the drinks, Kendra was boasting to everyone about having sex with Don seven days a week. In the twelve years they had been married, they had never missed a single night.

"Not even one night?" I asked Kendra in disbelief. "What if you're sick, or it's your time of the month?"

"Nothing stops us from daily sex. That's the rule in our house and the secret to our marital success."

We all stared at her in astonishment, and perhaps with a touch of envy. But then we all thought again, and looked at each other, making "ew" faces. We started thumping and hitting each other in a laughing fit. *Sex every night for twelve years? Even when Aunt Flow is in the house??* A definite ew.

Kendra made it clear that she would never share Don with anyone. Don quipped, "Never say never," and Kendra gave him a nasty scowl.

"Never MEANS never," Kendra sniped. "If you so much as touch a girl here, game over," Kendra threatened Don, pointing her finger close to his nose. Our laughing stopped abruptly. We were all sneaking uncomfortable glances at each other as Kendra morphed into a real killjoy.

Baryl interjected and said, "It's time to hear 'bout Stan and the Virgin Mary y'all." Mary's new nickname was both witty and fitting.

"Go ahead, call me Virgin Mary—that's fine with me. If that's the worst thing you say about me during the next few days, I can handle that." She downed her Eros. I took her cue and downed mine as well. "How about you two?" Mary asked me. "Tell us your story."

So, I told them about our relationship and our kids and admitted that our life sometimes felt "blah." "Are you kidding me right now?" Joe asked, offended.

"Oh, come on, Joe, you know our life has been kind of dullsville lately. It's no one's fault, and while this vacation isn't anything I would ever want to do again, it's far from dull. If nothing else, we'll remember this trip for a long time." Joe agreed, but I could see that my dullsville comment peeved him.

Then Baryl said, "Hey, why don't y'all come to the hot

tub with us."

"Sweet," Don declared approvingly.

Kendra, Mary, and I all said, "No thanks," in nervous unison. It would take a lot more than the truckload of alcohol I had consumed to take that leap.

I thought back to the pawing hot tub antics in the earlier light of day. I didn't even want to imagine what unsavory activities would be taking place in the dark. I shivered at the thought of myself surrounded by the crazies in the hot tub. Make that the *not* tub.

"Y'all don't know what yer gonna be missin'," Baryl said.

Whatever I was "missin'" was fine with me. We all said our goodnights and made plans to meet for breakfast at ten. Since it was almost three in the morning, we would be seeing everyone again all too soon. Joe and I went back to our room for round four, which I never in a million years could have imagined was physically possible.

DAY 2

I woke up to the sound of waves crashing on the beach, and a walloping headache! I turned over to Joe's side of the bed and was uneasy when I found it empty. No surprise to me that Mr. Go-Getter was up and at 'em.

What a way to start the day. I heaved myself up, popped two aspirins, and took a shower. I was lathering myself with suntan lotion when Joe came bursting in.

"I put towels on some chairs for us," he said energetically. "Julie, this place is sick. Wait until you see what's going down at the beach."

Sick is the last thing I need to see right now. This early in the morning, all I wanted to see was a steaming hot cup of coffee.

On our way to breakfast, we passed by the pool. It was obvious that people had slept there overnight. The deck chairs around the pool were teeming with men and women wrapped in towels. Two youngish, disheveled, brunette women sat up and asked us if they were too late for breakfast. "Not at all," Joe replied and invited them to join us.

I stared at Joe mystified. Within minutes he was jabbering with both girls and was the chirpiest I had seen him in ages. I wasn't sure if I should go to breakfast or run to the front desk to demand a refund. I rolled my eyes at Joe as the two brunette beauties chattered away with him nonstop.

As I watched them warily, the one with the cutesy pigtails noticed my unease and said to me, "Don't worry; your husband is safe with us. We're lesbians."

"Awesome!" Joe said, all hyped up as they introduced themselves as Tina and Candy.

Why are straight men so turned on by girl on girl?

When we got to the dining room, I stopped at the bar with Tina to order an espresso. Candy went with Joe. When the bartender asked if we wanted anything else, I was about to say *no thanks*, until I noticed Joe introducing Baryl to Candy. When Baryl saw me eyeing her, she seductively beckoned me over with her index finger.

I gave Baryl a hearty wave and asked the bartender for a mimosa.

"This is going to be a brutal seven days," I mumbled to myself as I threw back the mimosa. When Baryl blew me air kisses, I asked the bartender for another mimosa, convincing myself that my breakfast booze was chock full of vitamin C.

There were so many couples standing around Joe that we had to put a few tables together to make room for everyone. I sat back and took in the scene.

I still found it hard to believe that there were so many beautiful people in tiptop physical shape, all in one place. I recognized some of the couples from the bus and was barely affected by the fact that many had switched partners. After a full day of this place, I was expecting just about anything.

"I am never going to figure out who belongs to whom in this place," I grumbled. "That's the whole point, shugah," Baryl said. "Yer not supposed to belong to inyone while y'all are here."

I stared at Baryl in dumbfounded silence. *I'm so over this nuthouse.*

Baryl asked Tina about her relationship with Candy, who explained that while they were madly in love, they didn't have the courage to "come out" to their families. They had gone to college together and were both twenty-five years old. "My parents have their suspicions," Tina said, "but I don't have the heart to tell them."

Candy tearfully added, "I could never tell my parents because they would, without a doubt, disown me."

As soon as Joe told them he was a psychologist, the three of them stayed locked in conversation throughout the rest of the meal. Doctor Joe, who gives free advice to *no one ever*, was beyond eager to provide a "pro bono" therapy session to the lesbian lovers.

After breakfast, we all went back to our rooms to freshen up, and then to the nude beach. I tried to persuade Joe to sit at the prude beach, but he replied with an emphatic "no way in hell."

Oh, we're in hell all right, I thought wearily as we passed by a competitive game of nude beach volleyball like it was completely normal.

It was close to noon by the time we got to the beach. There were teepee tents set up in the water on floating barges, and dozens of inflatables in the shape of dolphins, swans, sharks, whales, and flamingoes crammed around them.

All of the floats had ropes, and a bunch of naked bathers were tying them up to one another to make one long connected row that snaked around the teepees. Some of the tents were open, but most of them were closed.

I didn't even want to imagine what was going on in the closed tents. *Nothing like a little nude tailgating to get the party started*, I thought, unamused.

Joe kept nudging me forward. "Stop overanalyzing, and let's pick out a couple of floats." I chose the swan, and Joe wanted a dolphin. As we drifted in the water, I spotted a shark moving toward us. Joe started singing the *Jaws* theme. "Dun dun. Dun dun dun dun. Dun dun. Dun dun dun dun." All of a sudden, Baryl's head popped up. "Ah won't bite. Unless y'all want me to." *Oh, how jawesome.*

Baryl asked Joe to go back to shore for an alcohol run, and he was more than happy to oblige. This was not the straight-as-an-arrow Joe I had come to know and love.

I surveyed the two of them and wanted to say no more drinks for me, but Joe was on cloud nine and gleefully paddled away, so I kept my mouth shut. This vacation was so beyond repair.

"Let's git ahselves a floatin' tent," Baryl said.

"Good idea," I mindlessly responded. Granted, I had inhaled my share of breakfast mimosas, but I was still lucid enough to know that "gittin" into a tent with Baryl was likely NOT a good idea.

There was ample space around the perimeter of the

tents to lounge outside. We hopped on the barge and sat with our feet dangling in the water while I craned my neck in search of Joe, who was nowhere in sight.

Inside the tent was a waterproof cushion the size of a mattress. My heart was palpitating so rapidly that when I looked down at my chest, it was vibrating. The tent flaps were open, so I felt relatively safe but shaky and lightheaded. "I need to lie down," I told Baryl, and I collapsed on the cushion. Baryl began massaging my head, and I had to admit, it felt phenomenal. There was nothing more relaxing than when Joe would play with my hair while we watched television. *This is not Joe, birdbrain.*

Baryl's touch was way softer than Joe's, and I was enjoying it but hating it at the same time. Before I could totally freak out, I must have fallen asleep.

Through my alcohol-induced coma, I heard a fracas coming from the beach. Baryl must have conked out as well, because we both jumped up at the same time and crawled out of the tent, squinting from the bright sun. It appeared to us that people were pointing to something in the water.

I sleepily gazed in the direction of their pointing and had to blink a few times to make sure I saw correctly. Baryl said what I was trying to verbalize but couldn't spit it out.

"Shugah, am ah seein' a mermaid strugglin' in that there water?"

Sure enough, there was an ethereal figure, with long flowing auburn hair, flipping and flopping in the waves. And there was no mistake about it; she had a fish fin instead of legs!

As I scanned the beach for Joe, I saw him dive head-first into the water and start swimming toward her. Then I heard shouts from the beach, yelling to Joe that the mermaid was fine, so he quickly changed course and swam to us instead. "The mermaid is fine?" I repeated out loud. *Nothing about this hellhole was fine.*

"She's role-playing," said a curvy woman matter-of-factly, as she floated by on a whale. We were all in a daze as this siren of a mermaid dove in and out of the ocean, all the while struggling to make it to shore.

I thought I'd seen it all, until a guy in yellow fisherman overall pants, trudged through the water, and entrapped the mermaid into his net. She was squirming around, trying to escape back out to sea, but he kept dragging his catch back to shore.

By this time, there was a sizeable crowd gathered on the beach, witnessing the outlandish event. After several minutes of floundering about, the exhausted mermaid gave up, and the fisherman hauled her and the net, onto the sand. She put up one heck of a fight. Role-playing or not, that part was positively real. We observed open-mouthed as he picked her up, still in the net, threw her over his shoulder, and zigzagged away.

The woman on the whale float filled us in, saying, "They come here every year and act out the same fantasy—hers of a mermaid and his of a fisherman catching her." Stupified, the three of us headed back to shore. The beach was packed with guests who had run over to catch the mermaid show. About thirty of us jaunted over to the bar together. The song "Castles in the Sky" was wafting through the air, and as I sang along with Baryl, I noticed the mermaid standing not far from us.

She smiled widely at me, and then spread her hands out toward her feet, like tada! "The ocean is the only home I've ever known." *Uh-huh.*

"But I have always longed to grow legs and explore the world of humans on land." *Wackadoo.*

I backed away just as the fisherman approached from behind and draped his net around her shoulders. *Make that wackadoo times two.*

I made a beeline for the beach, where a bunch of my insta-buds had set up chairs in a full circle. Sam informed me of his ingenious plan to go to the hot tub at 4:00 p.m. Ingenious. That was his word, not mine. *What was so ingenious about going to a tub?*

He explained that the daily rule of thumb at Exotica was that around 4ish, the A-list couples congregate at the tub, making it a fertile hotspot for hooking up.

As he was enthusiastically laying out his timeline for me, I was thinking: *Rule of thumb? Does Sam realize that the phrase referred to a seventeenth-century law that allowed a man to beat his wife so long as the rod he used was no thicker than his thumb?*

And OMG, using the word fertile and hookups in the same sentence, is so not right.

According to Sam, everyone knew that 4:00 p.m. was "hookup time" at the tub. *Boo Hoo. I guess I missed that memo!*

I thought the hookup comment combined with the rule of thumb topped off with fertile hotspot was off the charts, but I tried not to show my disgust. So why did I say "I'll think about it" when Sam asked me to meet up with him at 4 p.m. for some hot tubbing with the A-listers? Why, why, why? I was more than happy to leave all things fertile for Sam.

"I can't believe Gwen's here!" Celine called out, as

she charged down the beach toward a glamorous-looking couple. A tall, perfectly proportioned woman with waist-length chestnut brown hair, and a well-built ginger-haired guy were running toward Celine, with Sam in tow. All four were in an uproar, jumping up and down, hugging and carrying on like high school teens.

When they returned to their chairs, Celine introduced Gwen and Danny to us. "These are our best friends. They told us they weren't coming, so we had no idea they planned on surprising us. Danny told me he was still recuperating," said Celine as she tenderly patted his back and gave us all a sad face.

"Have you been ill?" I asked Danny. Sam chortled at the question, so I asked him what was so funny.

Danny hunched his shoulders up and down and glanced over at Celine. "Should I tell her?" Celine asked Danny tenuously. When he nodded *yes*, she told me that the last time they swapped with each other, Danny, who was having sex with Celine, hit her pelvic bone and broke his penis.

"Literally?" I asked incredulously. I didn't know what traumatized me more—the fact that she was giving me details about having sex with someone's husband, or the fact that she broke someone's penis! I'm sorry, but breaking a man's penis is just wrong. *Oh, and sleeping with your best friend's husband isn't?*

Joe winced. "I didn't know it was possible to break a penis." I simultaneously piped in with "Ouch."

"Oh, believe me; it's possible," answered Danny. "I'm living proof. I haven't been able to have sex for almost six months." Danny and Gwen went on ad-nauseam about his damaged penis and had us all in hysterics, except for Celine, who was openly embarrassed.

When Celine, Gwen, Sam, and Danny left for the bar, Sam waved and said, "See you at four."

"What's happening at four?" Joe asked.

"Sam wants me to do the hot tub with him," I answered skeptically.

"Sounds like a plan," Joe answered all bright-eyed. "I'll go with!" I ignored his idiomatic fervor and suggested we go to lunch.

Candy and Tina were sitting together, so I asked if we could join them. The entertainment staff was getting ready to put on a fashion show, and they were searching for models. Candy and Tina said they would do it, but I said a definitive *no way*.

When Mary and Stan got there, they asked Mary if she wanted to be in the show. Mary was reluctant but said she would do it if I would do it. Stan and Joe were pleading with us, egging and begging us on. Then the staff told us that we could keep anything we modeled, which was the clincher for Mary. And even though I decided to join in, my quick afterthought was that it wasn't much of a clincher for me, because whatever hoochie clothing I modeled was going straight into the garbage.

We didn't have time to eat, but I insisted on a cocktail, so I barreled over to the bar and asked for a bottle of champagne and some glasses. Then I ran backstage to get ready for my debut.

A few of the staffers were putting makeup on us and doing our hair. I felt like *America's Next Top Model*. Then we got to pick out two outfits each. I selected a suggestive and way-too-short black romper with gold studs, and a floor-length, skintight silver sequin tube dress.

When I stepped out in the romper, my focus immediately went to our table, packed with our tight-knit group. And even though I was uneasy, it calmed me down to see the crowd applauding and rooting for me. The catcalling and whistling would have usually sent me over the edge, so the fact that I was having such a blast blindsided me.

Before her modeling debut, Mary strutted her stuff in the dressing room in a lavender bodysuit, which gave her an uber camel toe. I was busy shoehorning myself into the sequined dress, which was so tight I couldn't move my legs properly. Plus, the sequins were rough as all get-out and pricking my entire body.

As I shuffled out to the runway, the team-Julie table got up and gave me a standing ovation. When Mary and her camel toe came out, they did the same. Then it was Candy and Tina's turn, and they paraded out, holding their hands over their breasts, in nothing but matching booty shorts and butt cleavage, to more hooting and hollering.

Backstage, I tried to get out of my dress, reassuring myself that if I got myself in it, I should be able to get myself out of it. I was finally able to maneuver it over my head, but it got stuck on my shoulders. My arms were straight up in the air, locked next to my ears, and I couldn't budge. My organs felt compressed, and the scratchy sequins were unbearable. I called out for help, but I couldn't see, so I had no clue if I was alone or not.

I thought I heard a noise. "Hello. Anyone out there?" I flailed around and then stumbled backward, knocking over a chair. The dress had zero give, and it was so tight around my chest; it was difficult to breathe. "I'm dying of asphyxiation here!" I heard a giggle and then a roar.

While my supposed friends thought my straight jacket was screamingly funny, I was in full-blown suffocation mode. "This dress is killing me, people," I grumbled as they snorted and cried. They finally grasped the top of the dress and yanked it off me. It took all three of them to extricate me from it. I collapsed onto the floor to catch my breath, while Mary, Candy, and Tina collapsed on the floor, laughing. "This dress needs a freaking warning label," I said, all shook up, which made them roar even louder.

When their fit was finally over, the four of us gave each other high tens, and Mary held me so hard and long that I was feeling awkward. Plus, I was still having difficulty breathing. "I love you, Julie," Mary said earnestly. I'm sure it was all the champagne, but I dotingly told her I felt the same, as we traipsed back to the table arm in arm. Champagne or no champagne, I was certain that I would be Mary's friend for a long time.

After lunch, Joe asked me to take a stroll on the beach with him. About ten minutes into our walk, the rain started pelting down on us. Running for shelter, we jumped under a charming octangular wedding gazebo built at the water's edge. *Do people actually get married here?*

We were in awe of the fierceness of the torrential rain and spectacular waves crashing onto the rocks beneath us. The weather was stormy, but at the same time, it all seemed so naturally peaceful and serene.

The gazebo was open on all sides, with a few chairs strewn about, and I was sitting on Joe's lap. I put my arms around his neck, and we sat there silently until the rain stopped. Joe gently took my face in his hands and told me he had never felt closer to me. "I will never forget this vacation Julie, and will treasure our time together here forever."

I got slightly weepy, and we hugged as if it were our last hug ever. We marveled at the irony that a resort all about sex, with an infamous reputation, could bring out such strong emotions of love. While I was immersed in the romance part of it, Joe, ever the psychologist, was pontificating that our love emoting was due to the intoxicating combination of out-of-the-norm freedom of thought and action, mixed with intense physical and mental intimacy. I thought Joe was going a little overboard, but our Exotica adventure did seem to be shaking us to our inner core, that was for sure.

Joe further theorized that our barometer of propriety and convention was being majorly adjusted and that our views about love and life were undergoing a tectonic shift. *Barometer of propriety? What a tectonic bullshitter.*

Okay, so what I thought was pure love was actually

pure lust, because as soon as the rain clouds dissipated, we went straight back to our room and had tectonic sex!

I awoke to Joe yelling at someone from our balcony. "We'll be there in ten minutes," I heard him say through my grogginess. "Be where in ten minutes?" "At the hot tub, where else?" he answered ecstatically as I stumbled into the shower.

At four on the dot, we were on our way to meet Sam when we saw Mary and Stan in a huddle with an exotic dark-haired couple. "This is Francois and Giselle. They're from France," Mary said, clearly impressed. *Yeah, so were the Coneheads.*

My French is horrible, but Joe's is passable, so right off the bat, he started speaking in French and flirting with Giselle. Her shapely legs were long and sleek, and she was bone thin, with a short Frenchy do and perky Frenchy breasts. And *moi* could see that Joe thought Giselle was the French bomb as he gushed on and on in his trying-too-hard French accent.

What I wouldn't give for a figure like that, I thought as I imagined my head on Giselle's body. As my thoughts and focus diverted from Giselle's breasts to her face, I could see from Giselle's Frenchy smirk that she found my checking her out amusing.

I stuttered and said, "I'm sorry for staring, but you're in such great shape that you must be incredibly diligent when it comes to your diet." What I really wanted to say was: *I find it hard to believe that a carb has ever made contact with your smirky mouth.*

Giselle fluttered her velvet-black eyelashes at me. It appeared that I had hit her skinny girl G-spot. "Merci, I sink you are too kind, but I don't have to watch zee foods at all."

How was it possible that French women could eat wheels of cheese, buttered baguettes, rich croissants, cream sauce on everything, gallons of wine, and never seem to gain a pound? I was going to have to do some serious recon and keep a close eye on what Giselle was eating.

When Baryl and David showed up, our gang of eight went off to the hot tub to find Sam. There he was, wearing nothing but a smile in the hustle and bustle, surrounded entirely by old people! And when I say old, I'm talking fossils.

A few of the grandmas were making google eyes at Sam. Make that the great-grandmas. He was trying to appear as nonchalant as possible, as he studiously avoided making eye contact with the ancient cougars.

Sam sheepishly covered his privates. "It's 4:00 p.m.,"

he mouthed, pointing to his watch and scrutinizing the geriatric pickins. It seemed that Sam was wrong—not *everyone* knew 4:00 p.m. was hookup time. And where were the A-listers?

Directly behind Sam, I noticed a mass of white foamy surface scum ever so slowly drifting his way. As the blob got closer to Sam, it seemed to grow in size. I didn't even want to speculate about what might be in that mass of yuck. Sam saw me pointing it out to Joe, and he turned to see what the hubbub was all about.

"Mon Dieu," Giselle gasped.

At the same time, Baryl stuck her tongue out in disgust. "URGH! What is that thang?"

Sam used the back of his hands to maneuver the floating island of scum away from him. But like a homing pigeon, it made its way back. As it got closer and closer to Sam, he jumped out of the tub and made a beeline for the outdoor shower, then reappeared modestly wearing a towel around his waist.

I was trying not to be snarky, but as Sam skulked away, I couldn't help myself. "What doesn't kill you makes you stronger!" We observed in wonderment as two frantic staffers attempted to evacuate the elderly from the tub. Baryl, Joe, David, and I tried to compose ourselves while

Giselle analyzed the situation. "Zee old peeples need zee anti-bacterien, no?"

We finally settled down and made our way to the beach, where several tables were set up with rocks and paint. Couples were painting rocks and then placing them around the resort. Celine wanted me to see the first rock that she and Sam had ever painted. As she steered me toward her rock, we passed a guy who leered at me and said, "Hey there, green visor girl, are you going to put on a show tonight?"

Show? I asked myself, miffed. Celine and I were trying to figure out what he meant. Yes, I was wearing a green sun visor, but I had no clue what "show" he was referring to.

We blew the creep off and continued on our rock journey. Celine guided me to a garden full of brightly painted rocks.

When Celine picked up her rock, she handled it lovingly and proudly. At first, I was going to say, *Girl, get a hold of yourself. It's a rock*, but then I saw the date on it. "You painted this rock five years ago?"

What I really wanted to say was: *The two of you have been engaging in these lascivious activities for five years already?*

"Yes," Celine answered wistfully. "It seems like a lifetime ago. We've had so many wonderful experiences here over the years."

I'm not sure I would ever use the word "wonderful" to describe the Exotica experience, but to each his own.

"I hope we stay in contact," Celine continued as she gave me a tight squeeze. "You have no idea how special you are to me."

I picked up a rock from 1993, and we toasted to rocks and friends forever, then ambled back over to the table where Joe and Sam were busy painting. Joe's rock was shaped like a lopsided heart, and he had painted "Joe Luvs Julie" on it. Sam's rock was painted blue, and it said, "Love to Tub." We chose a rock garden close to the beach and stacked them on top of each other, yoga style. Then we all had a cheesy group hug and made plans to meet for dinner.

The four of us were on our way back to our rooms when we came upon a couple pointing in my direction. The woman was exceedingly agitated, and it seemed that the guy was trying to placate her. When we strode by them, she glared at me and said, "You and your green visor better stay *far* away from my husband," as she huffed off in tears.

The husband apologized to me, saying, "You're okay

in my book, but my wife is not used to the lewd behavior around here." *Oh, and I am?* I thought to myself as I watched him chase after her. Celine inspected my head and said, "I don't know what's up with your visor, but you might want to take it off."

As we meandered toward our rooms, we noticed about fifty or so men and women gathered at the beach. When we asked what was going on, someone told us that they were waiting for the sun to set. The four of us sat down on the sand and watched the brilliant sun disappear behind the horizon on the water.

As I observed couples holding hands romantically, I thought about our newly formed friendships and the events of the last two days. I couldn't help but reflect upon the fact that in this infernal setting, there were so many free and easy, low-maintenance couples, who were authentically and unpretentiously in love. Okay, maybe they were in lust, but they were all unapologetically honest, and no pun intended, comfortable in their own skin, with or without clothes.

When we arrived at the dining room that evening, a talented pop-rock band was playing, and I noticed Kendra, Don, Celine, and Sam on the dance floor. Celine appeared to be conjoined with Kendra and Don. As the trio swayed, practically glued together, Sam casually observed Celine enjoying the threesome like it was an everyday occurrence. When Kendra spotted me, she came over and gently stroked my arm.

"You two are getting cozy," I said, surprising myself at the sarcasm in my voice. *Hold on a minute. I'm upset that Celine and Kendra might be hooking up?*

I had to admit; it bothered me when Kendra answered, "I know, I am obsessed with Celine. She is soooo over the top pretty." The look I gave Kendra prompted her to coyly ask me if I was jealous.

"Yeah, right," I answered defensively, although I wasn't sure what I was feeling. Maybe it *was* jealousy. Two days in, and I was jealous about one girl getting her groove on with another? I had obviously lost my mind.

Giselle and Francois joined the six of us, and I deliberately followed body-to-die-for Giselle to the buffet line, determined to eat what she ate. First, she stopped at the salad bar. With her face close to the bowl, she examined the lettuce for so long I figured something was amiss.

Just as I was going to ask her if everything was in order, she reached in, and with the tongs, took two pieces of arugula—no dressing. *Two crummy pieces of arugula?* But I followed her lead and likewise took a smidgen of arugula, and then promptly doused it in a shitload of blue cheese dressing.

Next, she stopped at the platter of fried chicken. Now we were getting somewhere. The scrumptious crispy chicken was topped with a few cherry tomatoes and some celery and carrots. Giselle gave me a side-eye as she scooped up three tomatoes and the six carrot sticks.

Enough was enough. I took two colossal crispy breasts and zipped over to the pasta bar. When I got back to the table, my plate was full of linguine with creamy Alfredo sauce, the fried chicken, and my paltry pile of drenched-in-blue-cheese arugula.

And Giselle? She was cutting up her cherry tomatoes as if she were digging into a juicy T-bone. She took the tiny tomato half, placed it on a piece of the arugula, and popped it in her mouth like it was a ham and brie on a baguette.

A half a cherry tomato and a piece of lettuce for dinner? No wonder she was a bag of bones. Giselle was irritated when I asked her if that was all she was going to eat. "Geezelle eez going to have zee dessert," she answered icily.

When Giselle got up for dessert, I followed her. *Hmm, will it be the black forest cake, bread pudding, or cheesecake with strawberries?* I went for the cheesecake. Giselle went for a strawberry. *One puny strawberry constitutes zee dessert?* Giselle was peeved at my dismissive attitude, so I backed off and headed for our table—but not before turning to her and shoving a fistful of sugar-coated churros into my mouth.

After dinner, Baryl escorted all of us over to the bar to participate in the Dirty Trivia contest. When I gave her an eye roll, she took hold of my arm and said, "Y'all are gonna have a real blast." The master of ceremonies gave us the lowdown. He would ask us penis and vagina questions, and we had to give the correct answer or take off a piece of clothing. *Oh, this is going to be a real blast, all right.*

He addressed his first question to Baryl. "The largest penis in the animal kingdom?" Baryl pondered the question as if she were competing for thousands of dollars. "A crockeydile," she said definitively. "Waaaaaahhhh," he said, imitating a buzzer. "Blue whale. Eleven feet." Baryl took off her shirt. Then it was Joe's turn to answer a question.

"The largest vagina in the animal kingdom?" "Female blue whale?" asked Joe. "Correct," said the MOC. "Their normal vagina length is about six to eight feet." *Important to know*, I thought to myself as Joe high-fived the guys.

Then it was my turn. *Yippee-ki-yay.* "Average speed of ejaculation?" the MOC asked me. "Tough question." Like

I cared. "Three miles per hour?" "At that rate, it would take a week to have an orgasm," Joe wisecracked. *Oh, you're funny, Joe.* "Twenty-eight miles per hour," the MOC said matter-of-factly, as if anyone who barely passed high school biology should know the answer to that one. "Like lightning," I quipped as I took off my earrings and gave Joe a raspberry sound. "Cheater!" my posse boomed. But all of us were trying to take off as little as possible, and since I was wearing a dress, my options were limited.

Mary lost next. And big time. MOC: "The average amount of semen in an ejaculation, is?" Mary was adamant that the average amount of semen in an ejaculation was half a cup. *Blech.* "Waaaaaahhhh. One to two teaspoons." We all made ick and yech sounds. Even the MOC made a yuck face. In a miniskirt and T-shirt, Mary opted to take off her skirt. She was wearing tight-fitting lace boy shorts, which showed off her toned butt. *Oh Lordy, now I'm sizing up Mary's booty?* "Come on, girl, shake that ass for me, shake that ass for me," Celine sang and danced playfully, imitating Eminem.

Then it was her turn. MOC: "What is the average vagina depth?" Celine: "The average depth of a vagina is eight inches." She said it with such conviction that even I believed her. "Waaaaaahhhh. Between three and six inches," said the MOC as Celine took off her dress. *Three inches is NOT a lot. No wonder so many women have that painful vagina thingy.* Celine was not wearing a bra and had on a tiny, jeweled G-string. Everyone was staring at Celine's ample breasts (including sicko me).

The MOC interrupted my gawking and asked me this: "How many calories in a teaspoon of semen?" Giselle perked up at that question. By now, a ton of people had crowded around us, enjoying the game and cheering for, who else—the guys. My answer of one hundred calories was wrong. "Waaaaaahhhh. The correct answer is five calories." As I mulled over what article of clothing to remove, Giselle queried, "Ooh là là, only five caloreez in za semens?" *Maybe Garnish Girl will add some variety to her diet.*

I had no choice but to take off my dress. Without a bra on, I was down to my underwear. "Darlin', are you wearin' bloomers?" Baryl asked me, taken aback. "These are not bloomers," I retorted defensively. "They're, you know, undies." When the laughing subsided, Baryl said to Joe, "Undies? Y'all need to bah this girl some thongs, shugah." She kept snapping the elastic on my underwear and taunting me. I was beyond embarrassed. So beyond, I thought about removing them. NOT.

When it was Kendra's turn, and she lost, she also had no choice but to take her dress off. The crowd woohooed and fist-pumped when the MOC asked Don the following question: In terms of sexual stimulation, is penis width more important than penis length? Don answered correctly: Turns out that out of hundreds of women surveyed, penis width was way more important to sexual satisfaction than penis length. *Important to know, said nobody ever.*

Then it was Giselle's turn, and she ended up taking off her dress and had no underwear on at all. The crowd was in full force, cheering the men on and chanting, "Go, go, go," with their fists in the air like obsessed sports fanatics.

I had to admit, it was weirdly entertaining, and my inhibitions were fading rapidly. I'm sure it had something—let me rephrase that. I'm sure it had *everything* to do with the fact that I was doing my usual share of overdrinking.

Then I lost again, and since I was down to my embarrassing "undies," I called an end to the game. The guys moaned, but we girls made their night when we decided to meet at the disco in an hour and then go off to the hot tub after that.

Joe and I went back to the room to change—but not before we had more outstanding sex. This trip was turning out to be quite a physical workout! *No wonder Kendra and Don are in such tremendous shape*, I thought to myself, remembering their narrative about having sex with each other every single day.

After our sexathon, we showered, wrapped towels around ourselves, and decided to check out the hot tub for a trial run before going to the disco. At this point in our vaycay, I thought I had seen it all, but when I arrived at the steamy hot tub area, I was astonished.

A writhing mass of well-oiled bodies blanketed the two tubs, and there was a torrent of mind-blowing, X-rated exploits taking place. I couldn't help but notice a voluptuous and sloshed brunette, wearing nothing but a visor, doing some down and dirty with several men. It was highly probable that what I was witnessing was illegal in most states—make that most countries. "Oh, good God, Joe, I get it now—she's the visor girl!" There she was, in all her bent over, green-visor glory. I winced and turned my back to the pandemonium and barked, "I'm out of here!"

My distaste spoke volumes to Joe, although *not* in the way I would have expected. "No problem with me. Let's go back to the room," he sensuously suggested in my ear, and my goosies got goosies. *At least this time, the goosies were for Joe and not Baryl*, I thought with relief. We went back to the room for, guess what? More glorious sex. But not before I shoved that green visor deep into the bottom of my suitcase.

We woke up around midnight and got ready for the disco. Only in the topsy-turvy reality of Exotica would we go out at midnight!

The disco theme was "Dirty T-shirt Night," and after rummaging through our stuff, we quickly concluded that there was nothing dirty to be found.

While I fished out two plain white T-shirts, Joe grabbed a magic marker and wrote "The Boss" on his shirt. I reciprocated and wrote "The Real Boss" on mine. When we got to the club, Celine and Sam were already on the dance floor. Sam's shirt said, "Chick Magnet," and Celine had on a glitter thong and a white see-through tank top that said, "With A Shirt Like This Who Needs Pants?" While racing around in search of Danny, Celine's friend Gwen was sporting a T-shirt of Wilma Flintstone, whipping a bottomless Betty Rubble. Sam explained to us that Danny was always roaming around, hooking up with people without Gwen, which would inevitably cause nasty fights between the two of them. Gwen was in frantic mode. "Where's Danny? Have you seen Danny?" I guess Danny's penis was back in business.

Baryl paraded over to us with boy shorts and a tank top that said: "If you're against same-sex marriage, don't marry someone of the same sex." In the distance, I could still hear Gwen frenziedly calling out Danny's name.

It was talent night at the piano bar, so a few of us left the disco to catch the show. When we got there, Kendra was getting ready to perform. We had no idea she could sing, and were blown away by her voice. We all shouted her name as she belted out "Bad Girls" by Donna Summer, cackling at the sight of her performing on top of the piano in a pink T-shirt that said, "Bitches Are People Too."

We sat around and had a few drinks until Kendra suggested we go back to their room and continue the party. I was skeptical, but Joe was begging to go, so Joe and I, Kendra and Don, and Stan and Mary left for Kendra's room.

As we weaved our way to their room, Virgin Mary was rattling off the list of things she was not going to do. "I'm not drinking anymore, I'm not taking off my clothes, I'm not going into the hot tub, and I'm not staying long. Oh, and by the way, I'm also not feeling that well."

Kendra and Don's theme room was "Cupid's Corner." They had a red, heart-shaped king-size bed with a mirrored ceiling, a grandiose marble tub to match, and a fully stocked red Formica bar. We were drinking and dancing, and I was feeling reasonably comfortable under the circumstances.

As far as I was concerned, the hot tub in Kendra's room had to be a whole lot safer than the scummy ones by the pool. Don suggested we get undressed and try it out. "Your call," I said to Mary tensely. "Oh, make me the bad guy," she replied.

"Let's just get this over with," I muttered and surprised everyone, including myself, when I stripped down and jumped into the hot tub. Joe was dumbstruck by my boldness. But from his turned-on expression, and his man bulge, I could see he was ready to rock and roll, as he promptly started to undress. Mary got down to her thong and jumped in with me. We gave each other a tentative high five, and Stan and Joe got in next.

Kendra leaned over the tub with a humongous vibrator in her hand and asked us if anyone wanted to have a go. Mary and I were numb. Stan and Joe's eyeballs were popping out of their sockets. It was apparent by Kendra's swaying back and forth that it was time for her to take an alcohol break.

"That contraption resembles a veggie mixer," I said, faking a laugh and praying that Kendra would keep it far away from me—and the water. "Wanna try it?" she asked me as all heads rapidly veered in my direction. "Oh please; it's all yours," I said back at her. Kendra was now the center of attention. "I guessh someone hash to get thish party started," she slurred as she wandered over to the bed. I clumsily got out of the hot tub and asked Joe to pour me a shot of tequila.

Kendra stretched out on their heart-shaped bed, and Don put the veggie mixer on her "spot." We were all awkwardly observing Don and Kendra in action. In a trance, Joe handed me the bottle of tequila, almost dropping it, never once taking his focus off Kendra and Don. I took a hefty swig, and when Kendra looked up bleary-eyed and blew me a kiss, I threw back another.

"Take it easy," said Joe as he took the bottle and mindlessly passed it to Mary, barely moving a muscle and still focusing in on the action. As Mary took a guzzle, her attention was also riveted on the veggie show. Don was on top of Kendra, and I didn't even want to know what was ensuing. Kendra motioned with her finger for me to come over. I was burning up from nerves, wondering what she could possibly want with me.

When I got to the bed, Kendra got close to my ear. "Handsh off Don, and that goesh for Mary too." I turned around to Mary, who was panic-stricken. "What's the problem now?" she asked in an urgent whisper as I catapulted myself off the heart bed. When I told Mary that Kendra wanted us to stay clear of Don, she gave me a sneer, saying, "Like I was planning on getting anywhere near the bed, let alone Don."

Then she clutched my arm and gave out a throaty gasp. Mary's eyes were as wide as saucers. I glimpsed in the direction Mary was staring, and there was Stan, standing next to Kendra and Don. Don was still using the mixer on Kendra, while she was playing with Stan's very erect penis.

I was certain Mary was going to blow a gasket. "Be calm, be cool, and sit next to Stan," I asserted authoritatively.

In a trance, Mary crawled on the heart bed and hovered next to Stan. Joe motioned for me to sit on his lap on the edge of the bed, where we pretended to make out. We were both dying to know what was coming next. So, with our lips smashed together, and our eyes wide open, we kept side-glancing at the bed, our eyes darting back to each other from time to time.

The scene was hypnagogic. Don was hovering over Kendra, who was having sex with her veggie mixer while simultaneously playing with Stan's larger-than-life you-know-what. Spellbound, I zeroed in on Mary, who was crouched next to Stan, in a semi-fetal position, with her eyes squinted tightly closed. I wanted to be turned on, but the incessantly loud buzzing of the vibrator, combined with Mary's cowering and my concern that she might blow that gasket any second, made it virtually impossible.

I whispered in Joe's ear and asked him if this jam session was supposed to be arousing. "Not to me," he said with an ick face, and put my hand on his private. Poor Joe was softer than a marshmallow.

Here we were in the middle of an orgy, but we were both thoroughly turned off. It was more like a *boregy*. I shoved Joe into a chair, and straddled him, pretending that we were all hot and bothered, when the truth was, we were cringing and trying as hard as we could to control our hysterics.

Kendra had the mother of all orgasms, letting out a primal scream while Mary, with her eyes still closed, covered her ears.

I had to cover my mouth to also keep from screaming—from primal hysteria. Stan was tensely assessing Mary—whose eyes were still cemented shut—certain that she was going to castrate him. I was hoping she wasn't going to be that mad at him, given the simple fact that she hadn't seen a damn thing.

"Anyone hungry?" I asked meekly after Kendra's screams had subsided.

Joe, Mary, and Stan shouted, "Yes!" in unison. Kendra and Don said they were tired and opted to stay in their room.

On the way to the dining room, I was weaving arm and arm with Mary, trying to choose my words carefully. "What the hell just happened?" I finally asked.

"Close encounters of the veggie kind," Joe replied.

The four of us proceeded to imitate Kendra's screaming, in an altogether sidesplitting scene. I was relieved that Mary was not boiling mad at Stan, but I concluded that she was so hammered she couldn't muster up the strength to be much of anything. We skipped food and gave each other a crushing embrace, promising to meet for breakfast the next morning.

DAY 3

"GOOD MORNING, SLEEPING BEAUTY," JOE SING-songed in my ear. I winced at his overly loud, get-up-and-go wake-up call. "We're going to breakfast and then sexy clothes shopping for you," Joe said boyishly. *Best day ever.*

I feigned enthusiasm and tried to ignore my swollen, alcohol-filled stomach and the shooting pains in my head. We went to the dining room and found our playmates huddled together. "Come join us," Sam shouted as he waved us over. I had never felt so popular—and hungover—in my entire life. "The hot tub was a real zoo last night," Sam said excitedly. Celine emphatically agreed and asked, "Where were you guys?"

I turned to Mary, who looked like crap as she discreetly moved her hand across her neck as if to say, *Do not breathe a word about last night.* Yeah, like I might. "We turned in early," I responded while Kendra and Don blankly stared down at their huevos rancheros. "You guys need to loosen up," Celine said with a wink. *She should only know*, I thought as I gave hangdog Stan the once over.

While the gang was busy whooping it up, I caught Mary's attention and did a subtle imitation of her curled up with her eyes tightly shut. When I opened my eyes, she had her mouth covered with her napkin, stifling a laugh.

After breakfast, Joe and I went to the boutique. He bought me a microscopic skirt, which was barely twelve inches in length, and a dinky black top that the saleswoman described as a boob tube. Real stripper wear. Then Joe added a pair of black short shorts, and a couple of see-through tank tops to the slut pile as well. Daisy Duke, here I come.

Joe was over the moon when I threw in a few thongs and a pink marabou negligee with matching kitten slippers. The bill came to four hundred twenty-seven dollars, and Joe enthusiastically handed over his credit card. Like Joe had ever willingly spent that kind of money on clothes for me before. In fact, I couldn't recall Joe *ever* accompanying me to buy clothes at all!

"I'm betting that your underwear days are a thing of the past," Joe said teasingly. It was more like my *clothing* days were a thing of the past, since what we bought did not qualify as much of anything.

After the shopping splurge, we went back to our room, and I modeled some of the clothes for Joe, prancing around while he sat at full attention on a chair. Joe must have liked the show because he pulled me onto his lap for more world-class sex.

At lunch, we bumped into Baryl, David, Kendra, and Don, and they invited us to go water skiing with them. When we got to the ski boat, there was a gorgeous young couple already aboard. They introduced themselves as Yuri and Olga and told us they were from Russia. Yuri seemed to be in his early thirties, and Olga claimed she was twenty-one.

TWENTY-ONE? Now we were getting into some questionable, possibly even criminal territory. *With the hardcore conduct that goes on around here, they should have a minimum age requirement of at least twenty-five*, I thought to myself. *Make that thirty. Holy crap, if any of my kids ever wound up here*, I thought horrified and promptly drove any thoughts of my offspring out of my head.

Olga was topless, with breasts that defied gravity. All of the guys were near-drooling. And some of us girls were near-drooling too. I'll admit I was copping a few breast peeks along with the guys. *My bad, bad, bad*, I said to myself in pure disgust. But that didn't stop me from taking a few more peeks and praying Olga was indeed twenty-one.

Yuri got on the skis first. Within a second or two, he was skiing like a professional: two skis, then one ski; one hand; backward; one leg up; gracefully twisting around in the wind. You name it; he was doing it. We were all transfixed by his talent.

Then it was Baryl's turn, and she was an accomplished skier as well. Then Don was up, and he was so handsome, tan, and muscled up that I was too occupied with his herculean body to pay much attention to his skiing ability. But he was no slouch. Then came Kendra, and she also had talent, staying up forever on the skis and doing her own set of tricks.

A slew of bathers on the beach and in the water were eyeing Kendra, and it wasn't just for her skiing abilities. Her tiny bikini top was half on, half off, so she decided to let go of the rope. Once Kendra got back into the boat, Joe was feeling like a macho man and decided that he wanted to ski next. "Joe," I reminded him discreetly, "you haven't been water skiing in over ten years."

"It's all good! I'll be back in the saddle in no time," he answered confidently.

I was worried that it wasn't going to be good at all

and that Joe might seriously injure himself. But based on the way he was staring so zealously at Olga's breasts, I was equally worried that if Joe didn't stop ogling and ski, Yuri might do the injuring.

The first time Joe tried to get up on the skis, he fell flat on his face. We all laughed uproariously. Then he tried again and fell backward, making us split our sides even more. "Getting back into the saddle" was not going to be as easy as Joe thought.

Then he tried a third time, and we all had enough of Joe making a fool out of himself. The guy driving the boat tapped me on the shoulder and asked in his thick Mexican accent, "Is thees the señor's first time?"

Yuri and Olga were getting impatient, with Yuri checking the time on his deep-sea Rolex, so I hollered to Joe, "Hey, señor, this is your last shot."

On the fourth try, Joe finally got up and was doing a sort of toilet bowl squat. We were all holding our stomachs, cracking up. The crowd on the beach and in the water were pointing and chuckling as well.

Then, all of a sudden, Joe lost his balance and hit the water. But he didn't let go of the rope, so he was bouncing off the surface like a skipping rock. No more laughing for me. While everyone else was in convulsions, they failed to see that Joe had disappeared into the water headfirst.

As the seconds ticked by, with no sign of Joe, I became frantic and started shouting his name. At this point, everyone on the boat was concerned. The skis were floating in the water, but Joe was nowhere to be found—not even a ripple to let us know where he might be.

Then, like a cannon, Joe shot out from the water and yelled, "I'M OKAY!" for all to hear. It reminded us of a Ben Stiller move, and we were all roaring so hard and falling all over each other that the boat was rocking as if it were a bathtub toy.

Joe swam back to us, and Yuri pulled him into the boat, with everyone still snickering and snorting. Both of Joe's knees were bloody and scraped. As he rubbed his knees while timidly eyeing us, we all shrieked so hard we were choking. Joe was embarrassed and deflated, but after a while, he finally joined in with the laughter, as he recognized the humor in his less-than-world-class performance.

When we got back from water skiing, Joe went to the infirmary to get his knees cleaned up and then took a well-needed nap. When I woke him for dinner, he tried to get up, but his back was so sore he could barely stand, so he told me to go without him. I wasn't sure I wanted to, but how much trouble could I get into at dinner?

The theme for the evening was "Pirate Night," so I put on the black short shorts and boob tube and made my way over to the Group Therapy bar. Many of the guests were dressed up as pirates, and most were barely dressed. One woman wore nothing but a fake parrot on her shoulder, and her female companion had an eye patch on what she called her "kitty cat." I was feeling vomitatious.

Baryl was wearing a red satin headscarf and a matching lace-up corset and thong, while Giselle pranced around in a ripped, see-through, minuscule red and white striped dress with red fishnet thigh high stockings and matching boots.

Dinner was taking place on the beach, so we found two long tables and put them together. We rehashed our waterskiing debacle and comically recalled Joe's failure to get back in the saddle.

The fisherman and his mermaid sat at the table next to us. Her flowing red tendrils cascaded over her topless breasts, and she wore a long, skin-tight lime green latex mermaid skirt. He was dressed in full-out pirate attire and had his net wrapped around one of her arms.

As Giselle nibbled on a celery stick, she adamantly declared, "Chacun à son gout!" *Each to his own taste.* If there was one thing I learned at Exotica, it was that everyone had their taste level. With that said, I found much of the vacation happenings to be très distasteful.

Although, it did turn out to be a blast of a night. I was carousing and celebrating with my new cohort like I was back in college. And even though I felt guilty about it, Joe barely crossed my mind.

After dinner, I went back to the room to see how Joe was feeling, but he was lying in bed moaning. Witnessing Joe, butt naked, and writhing in agony on Caesar's bed was rather comical, but I was trying to feel his pain. Kind of, sort of. "I might have thrown out my back, Julie." Joe was feeling the effect of having overdone it in his overzealous earlier attempt to impress Olga and her picture-perfect breasts.

Joe went on to say that he would not be able to make it out for the evening activities. I knew he must be feeling real real bad because there was no way he would miss one millisecond of Exotica action unless his condition was unfixable.

Joe whimpered to me to go out and enjoy myself, and he would try to make a recovery and join me later. And even though Joe got what he deserved, his pained expression and my spousal instinct kicked in. I reluctantly told Joe I would stay in, keep him company, and take care of him. To be honest, I wanted to continue partying, but I was unsure about how a trip to the disco by my lonesome would pan out.

But Joe insisted that I go. He reiterated that if he couldn't be out enjoying the fun, he wanted to make sure that at least one of us was getting our money's worth—the ever-frugal Joe. I was enjoying myself despite all of my earlier trepidations about the goings-on at Exotica, so after a mild pretend-protest, I agreed to leave Joe behind.

"Only two things, Julie," he instructed, throwing up two fingers adamantly. "First, don't get into any predicaments. Second, bring me back all the gossip. I insist on a blow-by-blow report!" Joe further blabbed on that he wanted me to indulge him—to *titillate* him. Oh, so that was it. If Joe couldn't be in on all the fun, he wanted a virtual night out? I was going to be his proxy at the evening's festivities so he could titillate himself later when I brought him back my blow-by-blow? *So gross.*

I glanced at him coquettishly while giving him an imaginary middle finger. *Titillate that, Joe.* But I feigned enthusiasm for his request, assured him that getting into a predicament was not in the plan, and went out to the disco solo.

Celine and Sam were at the bar with Mary and Stan.

Mary was tipsy and hanging all over Sam. Stan was in awe and loving every minute of it. "This sinful behavior coming from the V Mary?" I asked him, and we both cracked up.

Mary stuck her tongue out at me, then pointed to the dance floor. When I turned around, I saw Baryl and Kendra on the dance, aka stripper pole. Witnessing the duo body spinning on the pole was disturbing enough, but did they have to make out in front of everyone at the disco?

I was irritated that Kendra had claimed to be so prim and proper. *First last night and now this*, I thought to my judgmental self. But then I came back to reality—and the absurdity of my misplaced annoyance.

I was jealous of Kendra, who was, as they liked to say around here, "hooking up" with Baryl. And while Baryl was trying her best to hook up with me, she was simultaneously hard at work hooking up with Kendra, even though Kendra had earlier been trying to hook up with Celine. *Back up and get a grip on yourself, Julie.* As much as I wanted to deny it, I had a crush on Baryl. But now it was clear that Baryl had her sights on Kendra. I stole a peek at Baryl, who gave me an overly elaborate and demonstrative yawn and covered her mouth. *Excuse me, but was the bitch insinuating that I was boring?*

I'll show her, I thought, and said to Mary and Celine,

"Hey, if they can go on the pole, we can too." And to their shock (and mine), I took both of their hands and stormed up to the stage.

When we got to the pole, Baryl grasped the four of us and said, "Hey y'all, gimme some shugah." Next thing I knew, we were all grazing tongues with each other in a tight circle.

As we smooched away, the audience clamored to get as close to the stage as possible. But the funniest scene of all was Stan and Don's faces. Stan's mouth hung wide open, while Don shook his head in disbelief. The five of us girls eventually unlocked lips and gaped at each other, speechless. Mary wiped her mouth with the back of her hand and then suggested we get some air. As we wandered toward the beach, Gwen was issuing a mayday call. "Danny! Danny! Has anyone seen Danny? Where the hell is Danny?"

We sat at the ocean's edge, and Mary leaned her head on my shoulder. "I'm so lucky I met you." She gave me a peck on my cheek. I gave her a peck on her cheek back, and she gave me one again. I gave her one back, and the next thing I knew, we were making out!

It felt like I was having an out-of-body experience, and even though my brain was ordering me to pull away, the rest of me was ignoring the request. "What the…," was all I could verbalize to Mary as I timidly rubbed my lipstick off her chin. Mary was a pathetic mess. "Julie, do you think we're bi?"

"I stopped thinking days ago." Mary pondered my response. "Would it be sleazy if we hooked up?" *NOT* the comeback I was expecting from Mary!

"I wouldn't necessarily call it sleazy," I slowly enunciated, wondering where this powwow was going. "Okay, so, do you suppose it would be an okay thingy to do?"

My heart was pounding, and I wanted to say, *NO, I don't suppose it would be an okay thingy AT ALL,* but instead, what came out of my dim-witted mouth was, "Ruh-roh." By now, it was past 4 a.m., and we were getting more lethargic and drunk by the minute. I could barely keep my blurry eyes open.

"Let's lie on that hammock," Mary mumbled in between hiccups, pointing to one hanging between two palm trees. *I Yi Yi.*

Mary jumped on the hammock, and I took her hand and plopped myself in. The hammock turned over, and we both fell off, spitting sand out of our mouths in between giggles. Then Mary cuddled me and said, "You know, I would only try this with you." *Um, thank you?*

"I trust you, Julie, and I'm sure you're as apprehensive as I am about this whole thing." *Apprehensive?* I was wigging out. Mary helped me back into the hammock and copped a feel. *Houston, we have a huge-ass problem!*

When Mary started nuzzling my neck, I was shaking in my booty shorts. At least I still had them on!

Once she reached my lips, the only thing on my mind was if I would ever tell Joe I switched teams. *Like, NO. I would take this secret to my grave.* I was a drunken mess and way past regret. I didn't even want to hazard a guess as to what was going to happen next.

As I tried to ignore the quickening of Mary's breath, my blurry thoughts were racing between feeling conflicted and liberated. I was immersed and lost in the intensity of the moment as the heat built up between us. She nuzzled me with her nose. Her hair was a glorious tumble around me and set my heart thumping. I felt myself tumbling forward into the abyss. The effect of the alcohol, the excessively late hour, and the nerve-wracking nature of our activities were all beginning to have a serious impact on me. That was until I blacked out.

DAY 4

I WOKE UP EXPECTING TO SEE A MIRRORED CEILING. Instead, I saw the sky! I turned to my side, and there I was, scrunched on the hammock inches away from Mary, whose eyes were bulging out of her head. The sun was rising, and it was getting light outside.

"They're here, they're here," I heard through my foggy, inebriated stupor, as two men loomed over me. "Who the F are you?" I squealed, and then I remembered the "hook-up." I screeched in Mary's petrified face. "Oh my God, oh my God, oh my God!"

God was so not going to help us out of this one! Mary jumped up and gawked at me, then at the security guys, and then at her naked self. That's when it was her turn to screech. "Stan is so going to kill me!"

The mere mention of Stan brought Joe to the forefront of my pulsating head. We jumped out of the hammock, threw on our crumpled clothes, and scurried off in opposite directions. The sun was still rising, which meant it wasn't technically morning yet, right? I was swearing like a drunken sailor, and praying that Joe would be forgiving.

I fumbled for my key and rushed into the room. Joe wasn't there! As I sprinted around the resort hunting for Joe, I saw Kendra and Don with Celine and Sam. They caught up to me in tremendous relief. "Where have you been? All of us have been running around like maniacs trying to find you." I was so busted.

Then I saw Joe. His face was dark red, the vein in the middle of his forehead was popping out, and his jaw was in an ugly clench.

I couldn't recall ever seeing Joe so agitated. He tightly gripped my hand and said nothing to me as he pulled me toward our room. I kept telling Joe how sorry I was, but he was in an angry robotic mode. To be sure, Joe was not in a forgiving mood.

When we got to the room, he sat me down on the bed and loudly patronized me. "It's 5:30 in the morning, Julie. Do you know how insanely worried I was about you? I thought the two of you drowned in the ocean or were kidnapped, or worse—raped. Stan told me you both wobbled off together after some sort of group make-out session on the pole. Group make-out session, Julie? After an hour or so of trying to track you down, Stan was worried sick, so he woke me up. Thank God for the security guys who said they found you and Mary in a hammock on the beach."

"We must have fallen asleep!" My answer infuriated him. "You f-ing fell asleep? That's all you have to say? I'm going for a walk to cool off, and when I get back, you're going to tell me exactly what happened." And with that, Joe left.

I paced the room and tried to clear my head. How was I supposed to tell Joe what happened when I couldn't remember myself? Maybe it was better that I didn't remember. I sat down in a still-plastered state and tried to come up with a believable explanation.

When Joe showed up with Stan and Mary, I scrutinized her mascara-streaked face and started to fake cry, hoping Joe would take pity. Mary, who I thought was coming over to console me, whispered in my ear, "Don't say one word." I was vexed but took her advice as Joe came over and massaged my shoulders. *WHAT?*

Through my overly dramatic whimpering, and a furtive gander at Mary, I told him how sorry I was, and he kindly said, "Stop crying, Julie; Mary explained everything." *Mary explained everything? What the hell did Mary tell Joe?*

My paranoid eyes immediately went to Mary. "Yes, I told Joe and Stan how we drank way too much, and then danced on the pole. You got dizzy and needed to lie down. So, I helped you into a hammock, and then I guess we both passed out. I told Stan he should never have left us alone in the state we were in! Stan feels God awful." Mary was so sincere and convincing, even I believed her! *Damn, Mary, you're good.*

I gaped at Joe and Stan, who were nodding their heads in guilty agreement, while I made a mental note to tip the security guards for not mentioning that Mary and I were naked and tangled together in the hammock! *Oh wait, I forgot—we're supposed to be naked here. Duh.*

"I'm so sorry, Julie," Joe said as I struggled to straighten up my trashed self. "Mary is so right. Stan should never have left you two alone. How are you feeling, honey? Do you need some coffee or juice?"

I've no doubt crossed over into the Twilight Zone, I thought to myself, but numbly answered, "I could use some food." As we made our way to the dining room, I fixated on Mary and mouthed, *WTF?*

As I fed my still-drunk self, Mary explained the whole thing—or I should say she lied through her teeth. Who knew the Virgin Mary was so adept at scamming? Okay, maybe I couldn't call her the V Mary any longer. But the guys were all ears, and both of them were nodding sympathetically and apologizing profusely. Bottom line? Joe and Stan bought the whole whopper of a story. After eating, I begged off and went to the room to sleep everything off.

I woke up to a combo of incessant chattering and my bad breath. When I rolled over on my back, Mary, Stan, Joe, Kendra, Don, Celine, and Sam were hovering over me.

My head was killing me, my back was killing me, and my neck was killing me. But that was better than Joe killing me. Mary had miraculously saved the day. Hell, Mary had saved the whole vacation.

Joe kissed my forehead. "It's time for Foreplay Camp, sleepyhead." "Foreplay what?" I asked, wholly uninterested. I had just about enough foreplay a few short hours ago with the V Mary.

Don piped in next. "Foreplay Boot Camp. Everyone's been raving about the class."

I let out a moan and rolled out of bed. "Are you going to watch me get dressed?" I wisecracked.

"Sure, why not?" Kendra said as she put her feet up on a chair. "I brought some champagne and OJ for the show." There I was at 10:30 in the morning, stark naked in front of an audience of men and women, who four days ago were total strangers. As ludicrous as it all was, these couples had become the most intimate friends I had ever known. I was shockingly enjoying myself and felt like I had been part of this clique my entire adult life.

We all made our way to the aerobics room for carnal camp. Everyone was in the house. The Little Mermaid, Garnish Girl, Tina and Candy, and Miss Cantaloupe Breasts, to name a few.

The instructor was the manliest-looking woman I had ever seen. Her pudgy but highly muscled self was crammed into a too skimpy black liquid leather bodysuit, and long black gloves. Her breasts spilled over the top of the cups, giving her significant bra bulge. The head of fore-play gave new meaning to the phrase "butch dominatrix." She stomped over to a trunk in the corner of the room and pulled out two paddles and a riding crop. Sorry, but this was not my idea of foreplay. "These paddles are gonna keep your asses in line," she threatened as she waved them around.

We were all chitchatting nervously when She-Man shrilled, "Keep your traps shut, and pay attention to my foreplay fitness class. My name is Babe, and if you wanna stay in my good graces, don't F with me." Joe was edging over to the exit. "Where you goin'?" Babe growled. "To the bathroom?" Joe asked, hesitating.

"Don't you make a move," she barked at Joe as she approached him, swatting the paddle against her hand. "Is your partner here?" Joe was so intimidated that all he could do was weakly point in my direction. Then Babe got nose to nose with him and said, "I bet she has a duller-than-dull sex life."

"I think she's good," Joe said timidly. Then he bolted over to me and clenched my hand for comfort and support. Or was it for protection?

"What you need is some killer muscle tone," Babe taunted. "You can't properly satisfy your woman without it," she said, moving toward Joe, who was squeezing my hand so hard I thought he was going to crush it. "For great sex, you need killer glutes," she bellowed in Joe's face as she smacked him on the butt with the paddle. "And you gotta have a strong midsection to allow for vigorous PELVIC THRUSTING!"

Babe couldn't possibly have gotten any closer to Joe as she harshly followed up with, "The last thing your woman needs is for your thrusting to slow down cuz you're in shit shape."

"I belong to a gym," Joe responded, openly shaken by

Babe's verbal assault. I nearly bust my gut, trying not to laugh at Joe's cowardly demeanor as Babe terrorized and dominated him.

Then she moved on to Stan. "And when your partner's on top, she does *not* wanna pull your belly fat outta the way of your penis."

Stan was shaking his head like a true believer at a Sunday revival church service as he replied with an emphatic, "Amen!"

It was Sam's turn next. "And no one wants to see a pair of droopy man boobs," she yelled as she poked him in the chest with her crop.

"I do NOT have man boobs," Sam answered defensively, peering down at his pecs.

"Man up and deal with the friggin' facts," she snapped at Sam.

Unsure why anyone in their right mind would rave about Babe's class, I was planning my escape. As I turned to snag Joe and bolt out of there, Babe marched over to the fisherman, who was standing next to me and ordered him to do pushups while kissing the mermaid's feet. He immediately and enthusiastically obliged.

Then she took Don over to a heavy barbell and instructed him to bend over and do five deadlifts. Don was in his element, so he puffed himself up and bent over confidently to do the lift. When he got to the bent-over part, Babe soundly smacked his butt with her paddle. Don jumped up and blinked at us, horrified—his puffed-up demeanor instantaneously deflated.

Kendra had her fist in her mouth to keep from making any noise, and tears welled in her eyes. We were all trying hard to control ourselves. The last thing we needed was the wrath of Babe. "Keep goin!" Babe yelled at Don. "Whatchu stoppin for? A little red ass never hurt nobody!" Obeying Babe's command, Don humiliatingly continued with his deadlifts, while She-Man turned around and refocused her attention on Joe.

Slapping the paddle on her hand, she ordered him to do abdominal crunches. Joe reluctantly got down on the mat and starting lifting his torso while Babe pushed him back down with her boot. Then she squatted over him, straddling his upper body, her crotch inches from Joe's face, and snarled, "Do ya like that?" Joe turned his head toward me, helplessly, and I honestly couldn't control myself any longer.

As Babe shrieked, "Six more, lightweight!" to Joe, I ducked out of the room, snorting uncontrollably. When I turned back to Joe, he had slid out from under her and was crawling to the door. As I left him in the dust, I heard her squawk, "We ain't done here! Bend over for a final stretch, asshole!"

I didn't stop running until I got to the pool. I collapsed on a lounge chair and let loose with a resounding roar. When I scoped out the aerobics door, I saw Don and Kendra charging out of the class, their arms and legs flailing wildly about, and I completely lost it.

At the beach, after we had all settled down and recovered from our foreplay training, Sam suggested we play a game of Truth or Dare. Sam asked me to pick one.

"Truth?" I answered tentatively.

"If you could be with anyone here other than your husband, with no repercussions whatsoever, who would you choose?"

I weighed my options and stopped at Mary, who shook her head *no* ever so slightly. So, I offered up Celine, who beamed with pure joy. "No repercussions coming from me," Joe said, expecting what, I don't know. Celine scampered over, expecting a make-out session.

"My turn to ask a question," I blurted out, turning away from Celine to avoid lip contact. After my hookup with V Mary, I was *not* looking for a repeat performance so fast. But Celine was miffed, so I clumsily kissed her on the lips, landing mostly on her chin, and then asked her whether she wanted a truth or dare. She chose a *dare*, so I dared her to make out with Giselle. Better Giselle than me.

Celine and Giselle started to make out, and before we knew it, they were all over each other, rolling around in the sand, feeling each other up, and dry humping like two dogs in heat. That seemed like an opportune time to remove myself from the game, and Mary and I took off for the beach bar, making *eeewing* sounds.

As we beat it out of there, a motley crew started gathering around our beach chairs. One guy, who wasn't getting a good enough view of the Celine-Giselle show, yelled out, "Hey, down in front. We can't see back here." *Hey knucklehead, this is not Yankee Stadium.* Game over for me," I said to Mary as we swiftly looked away. Celine and Giselle's romp took "public display of affection" to a whole other level.

As we escaped to the beach bar, an idea popped into my head. I told Mary to keep going, and I would meet her for a drink in a few minutes. I then ran to my room and pulled the green visor out of my suitcase. When I got back to the beach, I diverted back to our beach chairs and presented the visor to Celine, who was still busy with Giselle. "You earned this," I said smugly. Celine paused her session with Giselle, wiped the sand off her body, proudly put the visor on her head, and promptly resumed her beach orgy.

After leaving Celine and Giselle to their voyeuristic crowd, I rejoined Mary at the beach bar for a well-deserved Eros. When Stan and Joe got to the bar, the four of us made our way to the dining room for lunch.

Shortly after we arrived, Celine and Giselle, still covered in sand, walked in holding hands. Celine went to the salad bar and piled her plate with lettuce. She had clearly been spending way too much time with Giselle. The two of them daintily ate their plants as I stuffed myself with a grilled cheese sandwich and two brownies.

Baryl stopped by our table to invite us to a drag queen show at the pool. The Exotica activities and events were nonstop, with one sexual exploit blending into another. I was exhausted, but not about to miss yet another wild and crazy adventure, so a bunch of us headed over to the packed pool area and settled in for the production.

Two prior Miss Exotica's introduced themselves as Heaven and Nevaeh, explaining that Nevaeh is the word heaven turned around and that the turning around represented the decision a man must make. *Alrighty then.*

They wore identical high-quality wigs and matching beaded evening gowns, and gave a hysterical lip-sync performance to the Diana Ross song "I'm Coming Out." When they announced the reigning Miss Exotica, he came out doing cartwheels and round-offs in a tiny string bikini. He was graceful and delicate and looked more girly-girl than any of us did—and he had a better figure to boot! We were all mesmerized by the show he was putting on, and even more so by his stellar physique.

He introduced himself as Denver L'Estrange and announced that it was his birthday. He interrupted his birthday extravaganza to pay tribute to his parents, who, to my surprise, were also at Exotica. Parents vacationing with their gay son at a sex-crazed nudie resort? *And this should surprise me because?*

As I looked over at Denver's parents, I noticed that they were not much older than me. The reigning Miss Exotica lovingly said, "Thank you, Mom. As far back as I can remember, you let me play with dolls, dress up in your clothes, and taught me how to apply makeup." He raised his glass in honor of his mother, and his father ran over and gave him a shot of Jägermeister. It was clear that his parents couldn't have been prouder. And although the whole cross-dressing gay scene was decidedly foreign to my traditional mindset, I had to concede that I was touched and deeply moved by the unconditional love that flowed reciprocally between parent and child.

The three Exotica queens entertained and amused for the next hour or so. They enacted a hilarious sketch to the Bonnie Tyler song "Total Eclipse of the Heart," each sitting on a swivel chair. Every time the phrase "turn around" came up in the song, they all scattered back to their chairs and spun around. All during the song, they would flip and whip around like Olympic gymnasts, then run back to their chairs for the turn-around sequence.

The spectators were going berserk, whistling, and shouting for more. Men and women were throwing money at them, and women were stuffing money into the front of their low-cut gowns, which stirred up the crowd even more. They were drag queens and clearly proud of it.

After the last song, Denver's mother asked for the microphone and gave a toast to her son. Or was it her daughter?

It was weirdly touching and reminded me that Exotica had presented me with situations I had never been exposed to before. Joe and I had always been middle-of-the-road, tolerant people, but I was going to go home a much more open-minded and accepting person. Exotica had changed me in ways I would never have imagined.

After the drag queen show, Joe and I walked over to

the bar and met up with Baryl and David. Denver's parents were there, surrounded by a crowd of admirers, and Baryl made the introductions. "Hi y'all, ahm Baryl, and this is mah friend Jewlee. Ah wanted to tell y'all that ah adored Denver's performance." I wanted to say he put on a superb show, but I wasn't sure if I should say he or she, so I kept my mouth shut.

Denver's parents struck up a conversation with Baryl, who told them that her daughter was a lesbian. *Baryl never told me that*, I thought, hurt and offended. But then I remembered, *seriously Julie? I barely know this woman!*

Baryl and Denver's parents were discussing at what age they knew their children were different. "Mah daughter grew up in the South, so we all knew that we all had to stand behind her, cuz no one else would," said Baryl, and Denver's mom agreed emphatically.

Before I could ask Baryl about her daughter, Heaven and Nevaeh made their grand entrance into the bar, to a rousing round of applause. They proceeded to fawn over Denver's mother, calling her "Den Mom." They filled us in about *Coming Out*, a new Off-Broadway show they would soon be starring in, and how fortunate they were to have their den mother. "And Den Dad is just as precious," one of them said as they both threw their arms around Denver's dad, each kissing a cheek.

Den Dad told us that Denver was their only child. "I am unconditionally accepting of my daughter and her friends. My little dragsters," said Den Dad lovingly. Den Mom joined in, saying she couldn't be prouder of him. Den Dad called him her, and Den Mom called her him. It was time for another drink.

Heaven and Nevaeh explained to us that they no longer had a relationship with their families and that Denver's parents had taken them in when they were teens. For several years, all three of them had lived at Den Mom's house in Nevada. *That must have been some interesting household!*

In the midst of all of us toasting to life, Denver arrived and gave his parents a warm embrace. He was near flawless up close. His hair was a golden color and cropped, but not too short. He had such delicate features that it became clear to me he was meant to be a girl. He was gentle and attentive to his parents, profusely thanking them for coming, then opened his birthday presents. They were one big happy family.

Baryl left with me for the beach, where a bunch of our friends were sitting. We all rehashed our lives, including Baryl, who opened up about her daughter. I shared with them that the mind-jolting experiences of the past few days had an incredible effect on my ability to be open and frank with my thoughts and feelings. The level of adventure and human connection I was able to enjoy at Exotica was like nothing I could ever do at home. We were all in agreement that, as we peeled away the layers of clothing, we were also peeling away layers of inhibitions.

As we sat around philosophizing, we saw Gwen frantically searching for Danny. "She was a lot calmer when Danny's penis was broken," Celine said earnestly. *If Joe ever pulled a "Danny," I would break his penis myself,* I thought, as I peacefully drifted off to sleep in my beach chair.

After my much-needed nap, Joe and I stopped by the hot tub at you-know-what time to see if Sam was there. Sure enough, there he was—smack in not only the center of the tub, but also the center of attention. A hussy of a brunette was hanging on his neck, and a busty blonde was tenderly putting lotion on his burnt nose. A muscular, hunky guy was slapping him on the back, and this time, he was surrounded by nothing but good-looking people. And Celine? She was in a deep sleep on a lounge chair. "Mayor of the hot tub," I said to Joe sarcastically.

After showering and reveling in another blazing red sunset, Joe and I drifted over to the dining room for dinner. We saw Francois and Giselle at the bar. As we laughed about her truth-or-dare exploits with Celine, Baryl came over and gave Joe and me a tight squeeze. When Celine, Sam, Stan, and Mary showed up, we put together a few tables to make room for everyone.

Joe excused himself and said he was going to look for Yuri and Olga. Mary sat next to me and took my hands. "Did we have a great time last night or what?" she asked me quietly.

"Since I barely remember what happened last night, I would have to say *or what*," I responded gently as I affectionately tucked a strand of her hair behind one ear.

Baryl gazed at us quizzically and said with a twinge of jealousy in her voice, "Y'all are gittin purty dern close these past couple a days!" *She should only know*, I thought as Mary and I glanced at each other innocently.

Joe came back with Yuri and Olga, and all fourteen of us sat down to dinner, blabbing, group-gyrating to the music, and flirting. The vacation was turning out to be totally different from what I had expected. As I thought about it, I could never have anticipated—or even imagined—that the Exotica sexcapades would be as amusing and entertaining as they were. We were simultaneously astonished, and one could say, even blessed, to have almost immediately become such fast and furious friends with so many sincere and easygoing people. *Okay, blessed may be going a little overboard.*

After dinner, Sam convinced all of us to take advantage of the hot tub near the beach. He said it wouldn't get crowded until midnight, so if we hurried, we would have it mostly to ourselves. *Now I was hurrying off to the hot tub?*

We all went back to our rooms, got out of our clothes, wrapped ourselves with towels, and went to the beach hot tub. When we got there, Celine was opening a bottle of champagne, and Sam was pouring tequila shots. Slightly paranoid about another out-of-control night, I sat at the edge of the tub with my feet dangling in. *Plus, who the hell knows what's floating around in here*, I thought to myself, staring intently into the water.

I guess my intense scrutiny of the tub was enough for Baryl to ask, "Pinny fer yer thoughts, Jewlee Pie." She had no problem taking off her towel and exposing her naked self.

"Is it possible to get pregnant from whatever is swimming around in this water?" I asked watchfully. By now, I was getting used to all the nudity, so as everyone laughed at what I thought was a perfectly valid question, I gingerly threw off my towel and eased myself into the tub. Soon we were circled together, consuming more than our share of champagne and tequila, and we were feeling no pain. I asked Joe to bring me a glass of water with ice.

When Joe came back, Olga grabbed the glass from me and said, "Let's play a kissing game."

Oh, fun.

She took an ice cube out of the glass, put it in her mouth, and then passed it orally into my mouth! *Seriously?* Olga wasn't much older than my kids! *So, so gross, Julie.*

I turned to Sam and passed the ice cube from my mouth into his. He then mouth-to-mouthed it to the next person. In between passing ice cubes, we were throwing back slugs of champagne and tequila shots.

I was beginning to feel faint and slightly nauseous, so I told Joe I thought it might be best if we went back to the room. "Not a chance, Julie; I'm having a blast, and I'm not missing a second night of partying."

With that, Joe turned his head and flat out ignored my dizzy self. So, I clumsily climbed out of the hot tub, wrapped myself up with my towel, and collapsed on a lounge chair.

I could hear Joe and Celine teasing each other in the background, and I wanted to get up and monitor the possible—more like probable—crisis, but I couldn't move. Everything around me was spinning, and I was so out of it that I couldn't even call out to Joe. It must have been getting close to midnight because I heard lots of new voices around the tub. The wild and crazies were arriving!

I was over-the-top anxious, and I wanted to get up, but the alcohol rendered me paralyzed. There was zero chance I was getting out of my lounge chair. Even though my head was spinning and my vision blurry, I forced myself to turn toward the commotion. I desperately tried to fix my gaze on Joe, who, by the way, cared nothing for the fact that I was on the verge of passing out. The truth hurts, but let's be honest: I wasn't even remotely on his radar.

I was annoyed, but after the shenanigans I had pulled the night before, I was not one to pass judgment. "No way, José," I murmured as Celine put an ice cube in Joe's mouth and locked lips with Joe way too long for my liking. *He is going to be so busted.*

When Joe unlocked lips with Celine, she was star-gazing at him, but to her disappointment and my relief, he wasn't even looking in her direction. I sighed and said a silent *thanks be to God.* My stress level and annoyance were slowing down until I noticed that Joe wasn't paying attention to Celine because the jerk-off was too busy staring across the water at a ravishing blonde with Heidi braids, wearing nothing but a beige cowboy hat.

I willed myself to sober up a bit and somehow managed to sit up to watch the whole thing play out. Little Miss Cowgirl, with her braids and fake boobs, was smiling and eye-flirting with Joe! And Joe was smiling and eye-flirting back at her! Then I saw Joe motion with his finger for her to come over to his side of the tub. I started to get up to break that finger of his.

Then, out of the corner of my eye, I noticed a leather-tanned woman. Her skin was the color of nuked beef jerky. She was afloat next to Cowgirl, and she thought Joe was beckoning to her! Joe was so obsessed with Cowgirl that he totally missed the wrinkly Shar-Pei lady wading across the hot tub toward him. As she moved in for the kill, her sun-damaged breasts were skimming the top of the water like empty tube socks.

When Joe finally realized tan mom was coming in for some love, he went into panic mode. I was bent over in pain from holding in my laughter as she waded closer and closer to him. I noticed our whole group was spreading out, giving her room to maneuver, and I chuckled in quiet revenge.

Joe turned around and blinked at me in horror. *Oh sure, now he remembers that I'm lying here, sick as a dog.* "Don't mind me, Joe. Party hearty!"

Joe bolted out of the hot tub, leaving the poor tanorexic in the lurch. Hurdling in my direction, he half-carried half-dragged me to the dining room for some coffee and food, flanked by our rambunctious and uproarious inner circle.

DAY 5

THE FIRST THING I NOTICED WHEN I OPENED MY
eyes was a note with a smiley face from Joe asking me to
meet him for breakfast. *Oy.* I wanted to go back to sleep,
but there was no chance I was leaving Joe unsupervised.
When I arrived at the dining room, Joe was surrounded
by thirty or so people, joking and sharing their vacation
antics. As each day passed, our circle of friends seemed to
grow exponentially. At home, I had a handful of friends,
but here I had an army.

As we ate, I noticed a beefy dark-haired guy swagger
into the dining room with a breathtaking blonde prima
donna. They were both wearing togas—his white, hers
gold—and they took regal to another level. Following
behind them were four dazzling nymphets, all draped in
gold togas as well.

"That's Toga Tony and his wife, Cat," Sam informed

us, answering our quizzical expressions.

"Wow, that's some impressive entourage," Joe said, focusing his attention on the five women and their close-to-nonexistent outfits. Sam explained that Toga Tony hosted private takeovers of hotels all over the country and had thrown some infamously wild and hardcore swinger toga parties. His wife Cat was a trust fund baby from Greenwich, Connecticut, and financially set for life.

"Toga parties? A little frat boyish, no?" I said, making a holier-than-though face.

"Make all the faces you want," said Celine. "Tony makes a lot of money hosting those toga parties. Not that he needs to work. Cat's got plenty of cash to spread around. His next party is in New York City—in our neck of the woods. Maybe you'll join us?"

"Maybe," I replied before I had time to consider the ramifications of what was coming out of my mouth. I checked out Joe, who was (what else?) vigorously nodding yes. As I surveyed the table, I saw that *everyone* was nodding yes—everyone, that is, except me. I had been riding out the past few days reasonably well so far, but a swinger Toga Party in New York City? Cavorting around in semi-naked Grecian wear, within a ten-mile radius of *OUR* neck of the woods, wasn't exactly what I had in mind for my next foray into Manhattan. A ten trillion-mile radius would be too close.

Toga Tony took a table next to ours, and Sam made the introductions. Cat invited us to a private toga party they were hosting at 7 p.m. in their suite. Naturally, Joe was the first to respond, with a resounding, "I'm in!" *What if I'm not in, Joe?*

Mary and Cat seemed to click immediately. After only a brief intro, they were chit-chatting like old buds. "What are you two up to?" I asked, trying to inject myself into the conversation.

"I'm in love with redheads," Cat said affectionately, stroking Mary's mane of red hair. I assumed Mary would be turned off by the fawning, but to the contrary, she was irritatingly entranced with Miss Fancy Pants (sans the pants). Feeling a slight pang of jealousy, I clasped Mary's hand and told Cat to catch up with us later. *Find your own BF, biatch!*

Our cabal met up at the beach, and we hooked up a bunch of rafts to a floating tent. As I relaxed on the barge, I noticed a local guy in a boat, hovering around us. Giselle told us he was selling "de la marijuana." She wanted to buy some but didn't want to do it herself, so she purred *s'il te plaît* to Joe in her pretentious French accent and asked him if he would buy it for her. *Good luck with that request, Frenchy.*

Joe is as straight as they come and has always been excessively strict about abiding by the law. I naturally assumed that he would respond to Giselle with a resounding N-O.

But like everything else around here, nothing should be assumed. Giselle continued to beseech Joe in her flirty, French-accented voice. I tried to keep my jealousy at bay. That was until Giselle leaned in close and began to stroke Joe's leg, her hand inching higher and higher up his thigh! This French bimbo was nerving me up.

Game over, bitch. I roughly pulled Joe's leg toward me in an attempt to extract it from Giselle's hand. But Giselle was not backing down. Completely ignoring me, she also pulled at Joe, her hand roaming up to the "intersection" of his legs. And with no clothes on, Joe's "response" was on display for all to see.

Before I could murder Joe, and as Giselle and I forcefully yanked at his legs, he bolted upright and loudly proclaimed, "Why not? Sure, I'll go! It's time to get this party popping!" *Get this party what?*

First off, as far as I could tell, we had been partying like the world was coming to an end, from the moment we crash-landed at Exotica five very long days ago.

Secondly, Joe popping? He is the most reclusive, study-bound guy I have ever known. Joe's idea of a social gathering is the two of us on our living room couch, me flipping through *The New York Times* while he buries himself in the latest psychology treatise. This obnoxious French trollop had taken over Joe's mind, and I was trying not to lose mine.

As Giselle instructed Joe on how to buy "zee drugs," I was wishing this vacation away. But whatever. If Joe want-ed to buy zee marijuana, who was I to stop him? As I was shaking my head clear, Giselle was smiling and stroking Joe's arm, giving him her irritating *merci biens*.

At this point, I was fed up and so over Giselle's pawing of Joe. While I wasn't keen on Joe involving himself in an illegal purchase, it was the lesser of two evils—drug deal, or Giselle feeling up Joe. So, I frostily told Joe to go ahead and throw his medical license out the window and assist his new girlfriend in buying drugs—tout suite. I figured once I reminded him of his license, he'd come to his senses and back out of the whole damn thing, given my warning, icy tone, and curt demeanor. *Not so.*

Joe enthusiastically waded back to the beach, waved the "marijuana man" down, and pointed to an area where they could meet up for the "buy." Joe's psychology license was obviously of no concern to him. When the dealer dragged his boat to shore, Joe huddled up with him for a few minutes and then darted in the opposite direction.

Where was Joe running off to? Joe answered my question when he looked back at me and yelled that he was getting cash. Mary shook her head in wonderment. "He could be a little more discreet." In his obnoxious effort to please Giselle, Joe was practically flying in the direction of our room. As Joe did his best imitation of a champion track star, we all cracked up when his knees buckled, and he stumbled, almost falling face-first into the sand. As Joe clumsily recovered from his near mishap, he raised one hand high in the air and called out, "I'M OKAY!"

Déjà vu, I thought to myself, thinking back to Joe's earlier water-skiing exploits. He was desperately trying to do whatever possible to please the ladies at Exotica and demonstrate his mucho macho side. I vowed to remind Joe later that he didn't have a macho bone in his body, and if he continued his quest to impress, he was going to severely maim himself. Actually, given his most annoying and obnoxious behavior, I was half hoping he would.

Joe came running back down to the boat guy, waving cash in his hand. Witnessing Joe buy drugs was unsettling.

When he waded back over to us, holding a sizeable plastic bag full of marijuana, we all gaped at him with our mouths wide open.

I was astonished by his naiveté. "Excuse me? Holla! How much weed did you buy? Are you insane? It doesn't take a marijuana connoisseur to know that no one could possibly smoke that much in a year, let alone in a couple of days."

Joe, whose drug-buying ability was being challenged in front of his French damsel, responded defensively. "Cut me a break. How would I know how much to buy? I never smoked the stuff in my life, let alone bought it."

Giselle voraciously eyed the bag of pot and then eyed Joe. "Where are zee rolling papiers?" Clearly, this was not Joe's field of expertise. "Rolling whah?"

Giselle took the outsized stash of marijuana from Joe and fished out two lone rolling papers from the bag. "C'est terrible," she said, clearly disappointed with Joe. "Mon cher, Joe. Only deux papers for zee weed?"

Then Mary piped in. "You bought enough marijuana for six months, and the weed dude only gave you two rolling papers?" *I guess Joe made a real faux pas.*

Once we stopped teasing Joe, Giselle rolled two joints and passed one around. It had been eons since I last smoked marijuana, but like everything else that had happened so far on this vacation, it seemed as reasonable as someone passing me a stick of gum. As I took a hit of the joint, I wondered how we were going to be able to go back to our normal, humdrum lives in two days.

After a few more hits, we were all higher than kites. Baryl was giving me a foot massage, I was rubbing Mary's shoulders, and Mary was braiding Kendra's hair. We were all enjoying the marijuana-laced afternoon when Giselle pointed toward the beach and spoke to Francois in rapid French.

As Francois squinted in the direction Giselle was pointing, I asked him to translate what she had said. He explained that Giselle was wondering if she was just stoned out of her mind and seeing double, or if there were blonde twins on the beach. I scanned the beach in the direction he was pointing, and sure enough, there were two fresh-faced blonde twins—nude, of course. "Yeah, I see twins. I also see that they have twin boob jobs," I said dryly as I gave them the once-over.

Intrigued by the matchy blondes, or more likely by their matchy boobs, Francois vigorously waved his arms at the twins, hoping to catch their attention. Apparently, our coterie of party animals was about to get larger.

The twins waved back enthusiastically, and they both jumped on a unicorn float and paddled out to our water tent. They were equally adorable, with identical blonde bob haircuts and twin boob jobs for sure. They introduced themselves as Tuesday and Wednesday. "Are those their names for real?" Joe asked me, discreetly.

Tuesday, overhearing Joe, said, "Oh, we're fer real. I was born two minutes before midnight on Tuesday, and my sis here was born right after midnight on Wednesday." We all chuckled and asked where their husbands were. Tuesday said, "We decided to take a vacation together, so I left the hubby home. Wednesday's not married, and, well, that's a whole other crazy story." I was getting used to crazy, so what could she possibly say to shock me?

Wednesday continued, "I'm gonna fess up and tell ya my version of the story before Tuesday does, cuz she has a potty mouth, and I would rather ya hear it from me." She proceeded to tell us that she had been living with Mandy, their older sister, together with Mandy's husband and their three kids. Wednesday ended up having an affair with Mandy's husband, and when Mandy found out, she kicked Wednesday out—but not before smacking her around silly. With no place to live, Wednesday moved in with Tuesday, her husband, and their two kids. The five of them were living in a trailer home about thirty miles outside of Springfield, Illinois. *Okay, I'm not as used to crazy as I thought.*

"Whatever happened to sisterly love?" Mary asked sardonically.

Wednesday appeared hurt, so Stan interjected and said, "Don't let her hurt your feelings; there's a reason we've been calling her the Virgin Mary." Stan and Joe laughed while Mary and I gave each other an uncomfortable they-should-only-know sideways glance.

"Wow, y'all could be on Jerry Springer," Baryl said. Tuesday piped in. "Yeah, we're trailer trash and proud of it, ain't we, Wednesday?" Wednesday responded with an emphatic yes, seemingly thrilled to be trash. *Yuck* was the only word I could muster up at that moment. Wednesday continued. "Tuesday isn't as uptight as Mandy," said Wednesday, slapping Tuesday on the butt. *So not normal*, I thought to myself as Wednesday continued. "Plus, Tuesday needs help with Tom sometimes, so I try to be there for her when she needs me." The implication of what Wednesday was saying was slowly sinking in on all of us.

Interrupting Wednesday, I put up my hand. "Put your story on hold for a sec." I scanned the disbelieving faces of the rest of the gang and queried, "Am I the only one who needs another joint before she continues with this lowdown?"

Giselle promptly took the second joint and passed it around, while Tuesday picked up where Wednesday had left off. She explained how Tom was a sex addict and insisted on "gettin' it" every night. Kendra and Don were nodding in furious agreement and reiterated that daily sex was the absolute best thing for a marriage. Tuesday made a face and said, "After a while, with my chores, and the kids and all, I get tired of his wantin' sex all the time. That's where my Wednesday jumps in to save the day."

Really? Not my idea of how I might want my sister to jump in to save my day. Tuesday chattered on, clueless that we were all freaked out. Well, at least I was freaked out. The rest of our crew moved closer than ever to Wednesday and were all ears. "Yeah, sharin Tom is a real hoot. We's like three peas in a pod, ain't that right, Tuesday?"

I turned to Joe, stupefied. But he was so engrossed in the twins that I could be drowning, and he wouldn't have had a clue. I pinched his arm and whispered, "You better stay far away from these two degenerates." And by the way, isn't it *two* peas in a pod? Call me stupid, but two peas in a pod work for me.

Off in the distance, the little mermaid was flipping

and flopping in and out of the water. She was topless, with a hot pink, scaley, fin-type bottom. We chuckled at the identical look of wonder she got from the twins as she swam past them.

On the beach, we saw Toga Tony and his entourage. We waved them over and signaled for them to join us as well. As they were coming out to join our party, most of the guests on the beach were staring at us, and I knew they wished they were part of our getting-larger-by-the-minute group. By now, there were thirty or so of us raising some serious hell. I wouldn't call it total depravity, but there wasn't a snowball's chance in hell I would ever divulge our escapades to anyone outside of Exotica.

I couldn't help but notice Celine and Sam ramping it up with Yuri and Olga. Celine eventually waded over to tell me they were leaving to hook up with them, and I asked her how this "hookup thing" was going to work. She explained that most of the time, they hang out in the same room together with another couple, but sometimes they change it up. For this hookup, Celine was going off with Yuri, and Sam was going with Olga—*to separate rooms!*

A wave of nausea came over me, and I told Celine that I could never be in a room with another man without Joe. *Let's be serious here—I could never be in a room with another man, period.*

"It's so much easier to be in separate rooms than in the same room." I wasn't buying anything Celine was trying to sell. "That way," she continued, "you don't have to see what your husband's doing with the other girl."

The marijuana must have been doing a number on my brain because Celine was emphatically waving her hands in front of me and asking if I knew what she meant. I was shaking my head *no* while Joe was nodding his head, *yes*. *Another yes from Joe?*

As Celine waded back to shore, I saw Sam helping Olga out of the water. I shuddered at the thought of being in a bedroom with anyone other than Joe. But Joe's pure delight, and the fact that he was still shaking his buoyant head *yes*, told me he had a far different view of the whole sordid concept.

Tuesday and Wednesday continued blabbing about their lives. Like I hadn't heard enough already. But Tuesday kept right on rolling. "It's real tight in our trailer right now with Wednesday livin with us, so that's why we thought up this trip. Tom took out a second mortgage and bought me an outdoor Whirlpool, the two of us our boobies, and this here vacation."

"What a stand-up guy that Tom of yours is," I said,

sweetly, concluding that if I never saw these fake boob bitches from Podunk again, it would be too soon.

I had heard enough from the twins for one marijuana-filled day, but there was no chance I was leaving either one of them alone with Joe. If Miss Hump Day could mess around with *both* her sisters' husbands, it would be a piece of cake for her to mess around with mine. I dragged Joe out of the water, and we went to our room to change for lunch. Joe wanted to rest for a few minutes, so I told him I was going to the prude beach to write in my journal.

As I approached the desolate beach, I saw an empty wheelchair on the sand. At the water's edge was a couple sharing a lounge chair. The woman was wearing a paisley headscarf, and it was evident that she was ill. As I sat a short distance away from them, they both eyed me gloomily, and she gave me a weak raise of her hand. I said hello, and she introduced herself as Melissa and her husband as Greg. The headscarf hid her bare head, but she still had a beautiful face. And even though her demeanor was fragile, there remained an aura of high voltage around her.

Melissa explained that they used to come to Exotica every year, and she had convinced Greg to bring her back to the resort one last time. She had been diagnosed with stage four cancer a couple of years prior, and her condition had been steadily deteriorating. Her eden green eyes pulled me in. But I could see that behind them she was terrified.

I was moved by Melissa's candor as well as the strength it must have taken to journey back to Exotica, despite her condition.

When I turned to Greg, I could see that he was devastated. It was all I could do not to tear up. "Live every day like it's your last and don't have any regrets," Melissa said wistfully. As we waved goodbye, Greg carried her across the sand and placed her back into the wheelchair.

I sat stunned, considering what I had just seen and heard. Amid all the Exotica revelry and raunchiness, and in the throes of a seemingly endless flow of wantonness, new friendships bonded, and a general sense of living large and in the moment, I had been hit with a monumental sense of poignancy and reality.

I sat on the beach alone, contemplating for a while longer, staring out at the clear blue water and watching the gentle waves roll in from the sea. Exotica was hardly the locale for quiet philosophical thought, but I couldn't help but reflect on how the ebb and flow of the water was like the ebb and flow of life.

I tried to pinpoint when the doldrums set in and when the magic in our marriage started to fade, which prompted my quest for a quiet, romantic vacation in the first place. And then I remembered back to just a few days ago to the confluence of circumstances that landed us in what I assumed would be a decidedly unromantic excursion.

But so far, it had all turned out okay. Seeking a romantic setting to jolt both of us out of our mostly insipid life at home, we never expected nor wanted to wind up in a vacation setting like Exotica—wholly alien to anything we had ever known. But oddly enough, it was exhilarating, sensual, and in a surprisingly weird way, even romantic.

As I sat on the prude beach, enjoying a few moments of respite from the frenetic Exotica capers, I contemplated Melissa's admonition to have no regrets.

She was so right. I came to Exotica kicking and screaming, but amidst the zany, kinky environment of Exotica, my sex life with Joe was back! Big time. There were sparks, and thrills, and eroticism, and a whole lot of mind-blowing sex. After years of complacency, I couldn't have asked for a better outcome. *So, throw caution to the wind, go with the flow, and live life to its fullest,* I told myself.

I soon snapped back to the present and remembered that Joe was waiting for me. I trekked back to the room and greeted Joe, downcast and wistful—certainly not in the manner he had anticipated.

I told Joe about my meeting Greg and Melissa. "They used to come here every year, Joe, and this trip will be her last." Joe was trying to be consoling, but he wasn't feeling it. He had not been there to see and hear Greg and Melissa, so he couldn't fully grasp what I had just witnessed. Joe was caught up in the hedonistic mindset of Exotica, and he was unprepared or unwilling to reorient his focus to more somber thoughts.

I could hardly blame him. We were on vacation to forget about the stress and pressures of life. So, I could understand his semi-perfunctory acknowledgment of what was weighing on my mind. And I reminded myself that Greg and Melissa, by their own account, had spent countless vacations in the free and—let's be real here—orgiastic milieu at Exotica. Moreover, Melissa had gone out of her way to remind me to enjoy life while I can. *Was meeting Melissa and Greg a sign?*

"Maybe," I speculated to Joe, "I was supposed to meet Greg and Melissa for a greater purpose." Joe was cleaning his sunglasses with his breath, wholly uninterested. "What if the overbooking and transfer to Exotica was a sign?"

Joe's response was to ask me whether his rumbling stomach was a sign that it was time to go to the dining room. I ignored his question and conceded to him that the trip was turning out to be an incredibly exotic, thrilling, and stimulating experience. I got Joe's full attention at "stimulating." And I went on to remind him that we had made more friends in five days than in an entire lifetime. How I equated meeting Greg and Melissa as a sign to partake in the Exotica insanity, was beyond me, and a definite theoretical stretch. Even so, I vowed to make sense of it somehow, and sooner than later.

But now it was time to get back to the reality of the moment, and anyway, it was time for lunch. Joe was, as always, champing at the bit to move on to the next Exotica adventure. On our way to the dining room, we saw Mary and Stan, and I briefly mentioned Greg and Melissa to them. But Mary and Stan were busy gushing about Cat and Toga Tony, their upcoming party, and what Mary might wear.

I decided to park my recent contemplative thoughts into the back of my brain and to further reflect on the meaning of my encounter with Greg and Melissa at a more suitable time and place.

Upon arriving at the dining room, Toga Tony was hard at work, passing out sheets and instructions to anyone who wanted to make a toga. Joe and I ultimately decided to make it easy on ourselves and bought togas at the boutique. I was leery about my skimpy gold purchase, but no regrets, right?

Meanwhile, I was feeling incredibly anxious, and I wasn't sure if it was my recent "separate room" discussion with Celine, my lingering thoughts about poor Melissa, the marijuana, my slutty toga, or all of the above. What I *was* sure about was that I needed to loosen up, so I told Joe I was going to the front desk to inquire about a massage.

As the front desk beauty went on and on about the virtues of the hot stone massage, I was in another world. Melissa's words, "Don't have any regrets," kept playing through my head as images of our riotous vacation kept interrupting my thoughts.

"The hot stone massage consists of traditional massage techniques." *Blah, blah, blah.* "The temperature promotes muscle healing." *Blah, blah, blah.* First, a sick Melissa popped into my head, and then a naked Mary. "Each stroke with a massage stone is ten times more effective than a traditional massage." *Blah, blah, blah.* Next, an empty wheelchair filled my thoughts, promptly interrupted by an empty hammock. "Miss? As I said, we have an opening in a few minutes. Miss?"

"Never have regrets," I mumbled as I envisioned Joe alone in a room with Celine. I swiftly shook my head back and forth, trying to eradicate the vision.

"Is that a *yes* or a *no?*" asked Beauty.

"I'll try it, but I'd like a woman masseuse, please," I muttered while having no regrets whatsoever about concluding my separate room fantasy vision with Celine breaking Joe's penis. *Sorry, Joe, no happy ending for you.*

I was led to a massage table under a tent on the beach, given a warm towel, and left to lie gazing at the breath-taking view. I was relaxed and almost asleep when I heard someone coming. I drowsily and peacefully gazed up to see—*Shoot me now! BABE!*

She raised her eyebrows up and down. "Yer gonna like what's comin," she said, and her words sounded more like a threat than a nicety. I was quite sure I was *not* going to like what was coming.

For the love of God, I thought as Babe oiled up her hands. I promptly rolled over to avoid any face time and prayed that her massage techniques would be better than her foreplay training session.

"I'm going in for the deep tissue method," Babe gnarled.

"I'm not that stressed, so a light massage is okay by me," I mumbled, choosing my words carefully.

Either Babe didn't hear me or could care less. As she

crushed the bejesus out of my back, I bit the life out of my lower lip. I was in severe pain from Babe's ministrations, and contemplating how I was going to politely let her in on the fact that she was annihilating my connective tissue. But then she said five heavenly words: "Now for the hot stones."

Babe started to lay the stones on my near-obliterated lower back. "AAAAAH!" I bellowed as she worked her way from my butt to my shoulder blades with what felt like burning hot coals.

"Settle it down," Babe commanded. "We're just gettin started here."

"Go F yourself, Babe!" I screeched, shocking both of us. "We are done, done, done here!" I hissed in her face as I jumped off the table, sending the stones flying all over the place.

As I lunged out of the tent, everyone within proximity backed away from me as I thrashed about, shrieking uncontrollably. When I got back to the room, I realized, not only was I buck naked, but my entire backside was fire red. As I leapfrogged into a cold shower, I caught Joe lying on the bed, trying desperately to mask his chuckling with a cough.

After dinner, we all hurried back to our rooms to

prepare for Toga Tony and Cat's party. I had a blast getting ready. I put on heavy black eyeliner—Egyptian style, the metallic gold dress, and matching beaded headpiece. Joe commented that, with my dark hair, bangs, thickly lined eyes, and gold lame' regalia, I was a Cleopatra doppelganger, although he did have to apply concealer on the red wounds on my back and butt. As I winced in pain, I swore that if I ever saw Babe again, I would shove those hot stones where the *sun don't shine.*

When we got to Toga Tony's suite, I saw that they also had a Roman-themed room, although it was much more ornate and opulent than ours, befitting of his illustrious reputation.

The room was bright blue and white, with a blue and white patterned ceiling, and blue and white columns, decorated in pure Roman fashion. Cat was exquisite in a gown of blue hues draped over one side of her body. The other side of her body was bare, exposing her breast. We saw Mary and Stan in the corner, and Mary oozed radiance. Her glossy, wavy red hair was perfectly tousled, and she was wearing a low cut, pale chiffon tangerine mini dress, with a sheer, floor-length overlay, and sporting some major boobage.

As the guests arrived, we all crowded together, and before long, it was standing room only. The longer the party lasted, the drunker we got, and the more risqué the scene became. There was a long table of food, and I saw Giselle mosey over and take a peek.

She was wearing a hunter green thong bathing suit, with spectacular red, yellow, and orange dahlias attached to it. She had woven a beautiful floral headpiece to match, and even I had to admit she looked otherworldly. Mary noticed me staring at Giselle and asked, "Amazing figure, right?"

I mock laughed. "You'd have an amazing figure too if all you ate was garnish." We both watched Giselle take a sizeable gold plate and place one red grape and an apple slice on it. I gave Mary a wink and a see-what-I-mean look. Mary told me she was going to get some real food and sauntered toward Giselle, who added a green olive to her feast.

I tuned out my French frenemy and reflected on how quickly the past five days had flown by. I tried to envision what our lives were going to be like once Joe and I got home. When Joe came over and asked me why I seemed so pensive, I told him I was reflecting on Melissa and Greg and the whole switching-partners thing. "What could one possibly have to do with the other?" Joe asked, confused.

I explained to him that meeting Melissa had reminded me of how short life is. We would be leaving Mexico in two days, and I didn't want to look back on our trip and regret anything.

"Regret what?" Joe asked, even more confused. *Joe wasn't the only one who was confused.* I was mentally mulling over whether I should share the preposterous thoughts that had been swirling around in my head with Joe or not.

Here was the thing: I had come so far in just five days, bearing witness to, and then participating in, carnal proclivities I could never have imagined in my wildest fantasies. And yet, it was all real, and it was all happening. And through it all, Joe and I had more than survived. We were having the best vacation of our lives!

While I wasn't on board with everything that was going down at Exotica, I was incredibly curious and felt sexually alive for the first time in a long while. When I focused back in on Joe, he was eyeing me warily. I took a deep breath and somehow found the courage to blurt out what was on my mind. "Look, in a couple of days, we'll be back in New York, and Exotica will be a distant memory. Would it be a recipe for disaster if we tested the waters a bit? Maybe it's possible to find a couple to have a semi-hookup experience with?"

But as soon as the words came out of my mouth, I began imagining all sorts of disastrous outcomes.

"What do you mean by semi-hookup?" Joe asked me, instantly aroused. "We could keep an open mind; that's all I'm saying." *Open mind, Julie?*

I could see that Joe was flabbergasted by what I had to say. Indeed, no one was more flabbergasted than me. We both gaped at each other for a second, and then Joe broke out in the mother of all grins. *Probably no going back now, big mouth.*

While deliriously joyful Joe ran off to get me a drink, Celine, who was angelic in a vintage off-the-shoulder white crochet tunic, flittered over to me and squeezed my butt. So much for Celine being an angel. At home, if anyone—man or woman—ever came within a foot of my butt, I would have thrown a hissy fit. But here, it was as if Celine had squeezed my hand.

Now that I had so courageously broached the "hook-up" subject with Joe, I next decided to ask Celine how her "separate room" rendezvous had turned out, in the hopes of getting some instructive action points.

"We had a minor mishap," Celine dished.

Let me guess: she broke Yuri's penis, I thought to my-self as she explained that after she hooked up with Yuri in a separate room from Olga and Sam, they all hung out together. "That was the mishap?" I asked Celine unimpressed. She then pulled up her dress and showed me a thick red welt across her left thigh. "How did you get *that*?" I grimaced.

She proceeded to tell me that Olga had pulled out a whip and informed Celine she likes to use it on her fave women. "So, she decided to *whip* you?" I asked, thoroughly grossed out, pausing for a moment to choose my next words carefully. "And you *let* her?" Celine shrugged and then bent over to reveal a few more welts across her butt. She saw the look of apprehension, mixed with dismay on my face, and told me not to be judgmental.

If I had learned anything from this vacation, it was *never* to judge a book by its cover. Or lack thereof. So, I backed off and didn't say another word to Celine. But I vowed that Olga and Yuri would NOT be on my list of semi-hookup possibilities.

Semi-hookup? You don't know jack shit about hooking up, girl. I sat on the end of an ornately painted gold sleigh sofa and took in the lustful scene around me.

It was getting late, and the party was getting downright uncivilized. The hot tub was full of drunkards who, no doubt, had invented the word promiscuous. Celine was hanging all over Gwen, and they were rubbing salt on each other's nipples, biting into lemons, licking each other's breasts, and throwing back shots of tequila. Celine had no qualms whatsoever of flat-leaving her new BF, Olga.

"Do I even want to know what you two are up to?" I yelled over to them, interrupting their unconventional soiree. Danny, who was miraculously in attendance for a change, zealously invited me to join them, generously offering up the salt shaker and lemon slices. *How about no,* I mumbled under my breath.

As I leaned back, I noticed an older woman, wearing a short pink wig and playing rough with a muscled-up, much younger dark-haired guy—on the same sofa I was sitting on!

I tried not to appear terrified when I heard him beg, "Choke me." I scooted to the very edge of the sofa and gawked at them, immobilized as this boomer jumped on Muscle Boy's chest and proceeded to, indeed, choke him! Her hands tightly wrapped around his neck, apparently turned both of them on immensely. "Don't stop, mommy," he muffled faintly. *Mommy? More like great-grandmommy,* I thought as I lurched off the sofa. Muscle Boy let out a warbled, "Now slap my face."

I rocketed over to Joe and insisted we leave. "Your

timing sucks," Joe deadpanned as he fixedly ogled two barely clad brunettes standing next to him, rubbing their breasts on each other. As I dragged Joe out the door, I heard the boy toy say, "Slap me harder, Mamacita."

As we stood outside of Toga Tony's room, recovering from the latest Exotica escapade, Joe brought up how excited he was that I was considering finding a couple for a hookup. When I tried to back out of my dumbass idea, Joe put his hand to my mouth and affectionately said, "No need to explain every man's fantasy. I'm *totally* in and so proud of you!"

So, I *totally* kept quiet about my having second thoughts about hooking up, and we agreed to keep the dialogue going. Instead of going back to the Toga party, we decided to go back to the room for our best sex yet. My semi-hookup suggestion had turned out to be an incredible aphrodisiac for both of us. Even if we ended up doing nothing, just the contemplation and thought of it was catapulting our sexcapades to new heights.

DAY 6

J**OE WAS STILL SLEEPING, SO** I **GRABBED MY JOURNAL** and decided to take a walk around the resort to clear my head and do some soul searching.

In my rush to have "no regrets," I had gotten myself in a real spot. As I plopped myself down on the deserted prude beach, I tried to convince myself that semi-hooking up with another couple wasn't the worst thing we could do. *But what if it was?*

I felt like I had a devil on one shoulder and an angel on the other. Devil: You have one more night here, and after all you've seen and done, why leave Mexico without the ultimate experience? Angel: Spend your last night catching up on some sleep. Devil: If something goes wrong with tonight's hookup, you can make a speedy retreat, and then make yourselves scarce tomorrow until you leave to catch your flight home. Angel: Move up your flight and leave today.

I went back to the room and left my journal and a note for Joe that said I would meet him at breakfast. I went to the bar, ordered a bloody mary, and prayed that I wasn't turning into an alcoholic. It was our last day in Exotica, and tomorrow we would be on a flight back to our kids, our jobs, and our complacent lives. Ironically, I wasn't entirely ready to go back to our mundane routine and kept speculating about regrets—and semi-hooking up.

As I polished off my drink, I argued with myself about what kind of last hoorah I wanted to have at Exotica. Maybe it was finally my time to "bust out" and do something that nobody would ever expect mild-mannered, parochial Julie to do.

Whether it was the devil or the bloody mary, I vowed to spend the rest of the vacation enjoying myself, even though the mere thought of it made my heart race with trepidation.

When Joe showed up for breakfast, I decided to throw caution to the wind and shared some of my thoughts with him. I reiterated to Joe that we should keep our options open regarding the next twenty-four hours. *I guess the devil won.* Or, maybe there was some high-risk, high-jinx adventure hiding deep inside Julie after all!

"You'll get no argument from me," Joe said enthusiastically as we cruised over to a table full of our new buds. After we ate, we all settled down at the beach and shared our thoughts about life, love, jobs, kids, sports, sex—you name it, we opened up about it.

After we concluded our morning philosophy session, I took in the beach scene, scoured around from couple to couple, wondering to myself if any of them would be right for our maiden hookup.

At the bar, I sipped on an Eros and continued scoping out couples. I introduced myself to an appealing twosome sitting a few seats away from me. As we bantered back and forth, Joe walked over and pulled me aside. "And you're conversating with this couple because?" "We might be running out of time, Joe." *Breathe, Julie. Breathe.* "On this vacation or in our lives?" Joe asked, working himself into a hopeful frenzy. He was so hepped up I didn't have the heart to back down. "Both," I bravely answered, and walked him over to the couple I had just met. Well, I walked; Joe skadoodled. *I'm totally screwed, no pun intended.*

A few minutes into the conversation, we got the scoop. As it turned out, the woman was transgender. She didn't have me at hello. Joe couldn't get out of there fast enough, and to be honest, I got out of there even faster than Joe. Living life to its fullest was going to be harder than I thought. It was undoubtedly going to take more than a few days to undo a lifetime of prudishness.

Before we left the bar, we met yet another couple, who made it clear that their "thing" was for the wife to find a well-hung black guy to have sex with—while her husband watched. I interjected with, "Peripherally, right?" as they matter-of-factly agreed. They further explained that it was a rare day that they didn't find a black guy who couldn't "blow her back out." And although we weren't their thing, they invited us to join in on the fun. Blowing my back out was not my idea of a fun way to end our vacation. We thanked them profusely and bolted for the dining room.

On the way to lunch, we passed by the front desk and observed a new wave of guests checking in. Except for a few chubettes at the hot tub, we continued to be astonished by the endless multitude of in-shape people. But it looked like that was about to change.   The group at the counter was part of "The Big Women Who Love Big Men" club. An obnoxious couple in the lobby snarkily commented to us that being naked for the biggies shouldn't be optional. It should be banned. *Ouch.*

I icily replied that no one should apologize for their lifestyle, existence, or size. A member of the Big Couple club who overheard the conversation lifted me off my feet and twirled me around, while profusely thanking me. Joe rolled his eyes. "Now you're the spokesman for the big people?" "Spokesperson," I retorted sarcastically.

At lunch, Joe and I took turns commenting on the couples coming into the dining room. We agreed that there was no harm in "just looking." As the big-women-who-love-big-men group trucked in, they took turns fist-bumping me. *Who knew I would be Exotica's head honcho for the big peep contingent?* After piling hordes of fried fish and rice on their plates, they smiled and winked flirtatiously at us, while Joe kept kicking me under the table. I gave Joe a swift kick back as I scoped the place out. I had my own fish to fry.

I noticed a promising couple sitting next to us. When the woman walked over to the pasta station, I followed close behind her in line. But her perfume was so overpowering it permeated my air space, and I went into a near anaphylactic coughing and sneezing fit. *Less is more*, I thought as I wheezed my way back to the table to blow my nose and throw back some water.

When the mermaid and her fisherman came in, I glanced at Joe, whose face was as contorted as mine. No words were necessary. Then Francois and Giselle came in, and I mouthed *no way* to Joe. Yuri and Olga waved to us, and Joe gave me a what-do-you-think face—until I told him about Celine's whip welts. Double nada to Yuri and Olga.

When Kendra and Don dropped by to invite us on a "nude booze cruise" with them, we both said *yes* and planned to meet at the dock in an hour. Saying *yes* to a "nude booze cruise" defied all logic, but I was evidently way past logical at this point. "What about Kendra and Don?" Joe asked, interrupting my self-observation. We considered it for a split second and simultaneously said, "Nah." We had zero interest in competing with a veggie mixer. Plus, there was no doubt that Kendra would flip her lid if Don so much as thought about another woman.

The nude dress code made changing for the cruise a breeze. We were looking forward to spending a relaxing day socializing with our new peeps and agreed it would be harmless to scope out possible hookup couples while cruising and boozing. "Who knows? We might end our vacation with a bang," Joe said, emboldened by our game plan. I wanted to tell him to tone it down, but what was the point? After all, it had been my stupid-ass idea.

As we boarded the boat, we met Justine, a slinky, bosomy brunette who kept rubbing her boobs all over Joe.

I'd better keep my eye on this nympho, I thought to myself. Since Joe has always been a breast man, it came as no surprise to me that he and Justine hit it off from the get-go. I wasn't crazy about leaving the two of them alone, but I noticed an attractive couple at the bar. Even though it was hard to fathom, I was on a hookup mission. *Julie can-do!* I turned away from Joe and Justine and took a seat at the bar. I was politely engaging in small talk with the couple, but my mind *and* eagle eyes were on Joe and Justine glued together. *Time to separate the beauty from the two-timing beast.* Plus, the guy's hair was stiff in the front like a cockatoo, and he had supremely lousy breath.

I sped over to Joe and steered him away from Justine. We stood by the edge of the bar, exchanging our opinions about the different couples—and rating them on a scale of one to ten. Discussing the sexual attributes of others with Joe seemed outlandishly weird, but we were oddly enjoying ourselves. Plus, I was up for anything that would keep Joe away from Justine.

We both glanced back at the couple I had earlier written off. "The guy looks like a stud," Joe said authoritatively. *Please, Joe, your stud talk is so turning me off.* "He has breath like a dead elephant," I replied, smiling and waving to the couple as she blew me a kiss. "So, I take dead-elephant breath to mean he's a *one*?" Joe queried, scoping out the room.

There was a lull in our conversation until he casually asked, "What about Justine?" *Justine? You dirty dog.* As I gave Joe the evilest of all evil eyes, he asked if he was to take my voodoo eyes as a no. *F you, Joe.*

Then we spotted a couple at the bar who seemed like they might be a possibility, so we cruised over to get a drink. The guy was good-looking—until he opened his mouth. He first turned to Joe and said, "My little lady could use a good porkin. And then he turned to me. You gotta fine lookin knish." I was dumb-founded. "I'm pregnant," I responded. *That should shut him the hell up.* "I'm good with that," he eagerly replied. NEXT!

Still, we did not give up. Like two social butterflies, we secretly interviewed couples. One guy had a horrific cold, so I high-tailed it out of there. *A definitive one out of ten.* Another couple was so sunburned that their skin was literally peeling off of them. *No thanks.* One man who was bi kept referring to Joe's ass as a fine-looking toilet. *Run.* One woman had a ginormous cold sore on her lip. *Run, run.*

A hulking 6-foot muscle man full blast bellowed into my ear that he thought Joe was his type. *Well, that's fine, but there's no need to shout.*

We finally thought we were getting somewhere with a classy looking duo at the bar—until Joe whispered in my ear that the woman wanted him to insert a lollipop into her vagina and then eat it. *So much for classy.* It was one disaster after another.

Joe approached a possible couple. "Excuse me, hi. I'm Joe, and this is my wife, Julie." The girl smiled at us with a chock full of implanted halo-white teeth, that were way too big for her mouth, while the guy gave us their low down.

"We're looking to get it on with a couple who respects us enough to tell us what's up. If you're not feeling us, we deserve to know. Keep it real. Do the right thing and be straight shooters. If you lose feelings for us, don't lead us on. And we beg you—don't make us feel like assholes." *Getting it on with these two moe-moe's might seem like a great idea. For someone. Back away very slowly, Julie.*

Next, we chatted up a long-haired guy and his bohemian girlfriend. As he flipped his hair out of his face, he sang my praises to Joe. "Your wife is rad smart. We talked international politics A to Z." I bobbed my head up and down like I was agreeing, but I was thinking: *"Talking politics to Dumbo was more like A to B."*

Then two guys approached me. "Tell me about your-self," I asked guy number one, who spoke non-stop about his childhood. When he got to the part about burning his penis on a radiator when he was five, I pretended to care and turned to guy number two. "And what's up with you?" He pointed finger guns at me and said: "I've got a condom for what's up." I excused myself and went to the bath-room—but not before I told Joe to carry on. I couldn't say whether or not anything would come of our mission, but we were having a lot of laughs in the process.

While I was in the bathroom line, I met Raven, who had full sultry lips, a midnight black ponytail, dramatic false eyelashes, and a full face of heavy stage makeup, even though it was easily 100 degrees. When I asked Raven where her husband was, she said she was single. What I really wanted to ask was whether Raven was her given name, but I thought better of it. *Who in their right mind would name their child after a bird who eats the flesh of dead carcasses?* She went on to say that she had hooked up with this older guy about two weeks prior, and he offered to take her on vacation. Raven had no idea where they were going, but he had money, so she didn't care where he took her. *Didn't anyone ever warn her about stranger danger?*

She yakety-yakked about his money and seemed

overly obsessed with it. Raven explained that his name was Frank, but he was known at Exotica as Captain because he owned a multi-million-dollar yacht, which he docked there for several months at a time. *Hmmm, maybe a semi-hookup possibility?* My eyes searched around until I finally zoomed in on Joe, leaning against the bar. Whew. I was starting to worry that Joe was pulling a Danny. I told Raven to meet up with us when the Captain showed up.

Joe was quietly nursing a beer. Since Joe rarely drinks, I found it odd. He proceeded to tell me that he ordered a drink while he was waiting for me and struck up a conversation with a model sitting next to him. "I thought I was getting somewhere until she wagged her finger in my face and told me the only way that I was hooking up with her was in my dreams," he said dejectedly. I laughed it off, but she had clearly hurt his feelings, not to mention his ego. I felt a sting of jealousy from his reaction, and I wasn't sure if I should feel sorry for him or relieved. *Sorry, not sorry.*

My back-and-forth attitude about hooking up was incredibly confusing, and getting more complicated by the couple. Did I have the guts to go to the dark side? The new Julie was saying *why the hell not*, and the old Julie was screaming *hell no, no, no!*

Raven shimmied over, and I was semi-enjoying her

flirting session with Joe. *Could Raven be the one?* It seemed like new Julie was winning, and that hell was where I was headed. Hell, or no hell, I was thoroughly immersed in the dalliance—until Captain Frank showed up.

Then I began to gag reflexively. The Captain had a sizable paunch and was close to my dad's age. As I continued to observe him, I concluded that my dad was younger and unquestionably better looking. Frank was wearing a ridiculous captain's hat and had a fat cigar hanging from his lips. When he opened his mouth, his teeth were canary yellow. I wasn't sure what turned my stomach more: his smelly cigar breath or the color of his teeth. Money or no money, this guy was a minus zero. As we hurriedly excused ourselves, I told Joe that we should revisit the whole hook-up idea.

Joe gave me his authoritative face and said, "Don't give up yet. It's all about chemistry. Good chemistry equals spending more time together; bad chemistry equals keep on looking." *Keep talking out of your ass, Joe.*

We continued to make our way around the bar, meeting myriad couples, but no one seemed right. I had to admit, I was relieved.

As we discussed our disappointing and failed venture, Mary and Stan showed up. I stared at Joe, and he stared back. *Was he thinking what I was thinking?* Sure, it made sense—more than Joe even knew. I could trust Mary, and Stan was a stand-up kind of guy. Plus, we had already spent an enormous amount of time together, knew all sorts of personal things about them, and had become surprisingly close. And aside from their good looks, there was definite chemistry. *Holy shit, am I rationalizing a hookup with Mary and Stan?*

The first thing I learned in chemistry class was to be careful not to blow anything up. Would Mary and Stan go for it, or would we blow up our brand-new friendship? Before I could say anything to Joe, the twins came up to us. We would have to leave the Mary-and-Stan discussion for later. Tuesday and Wednesday took a gander at Captain Frank with Raven, and both made a synchronized yuck face.

Even their facial expressions were identical. We covered our mouths to keep from laughing when Tuesday said straight-faced, "I love what he's done with what's left of his hair. But how did he get it to come out of one nostril like that?" As I took a closer look at the Captain, Tuesday was correct—he did have more hair in his nostrils than on the top of his head.

Then Celine and Sam came over and started telling

us about Captain Frank. "He'll sleep with anyone with a pulse, and a pulse is optional," Celine deadpanned. She continued to amuse us as she went around the boat, making her observations about the various men and women on the cruise, with the twins acting as her backup comedians.

There was an extensive smorgasbord of pepper poppers, guacamole, fresh tortilla chips, refried beans, and spicy beef and chicken fajitas. People were piling their plates and stuffing their faces. *Wake up, people—we're nude here. Am I the only one concerned about abdominal bloating or worse?*

After an hour of cruising, the boat anchored near a mountainside full of postcard-perfect grottoes and caves. A steep slide was attached to the side of the boat so the guests could access the water. Joe said he was going for a swim, and I wanted to join him. But after three Eros drinks, his opinion was that I was in no condition to go in the water, and I agreed.

Call me paranoid, but Joe seemed deliriously happy that I wouldn't be joining him. His lips barely grazed my cheek, and he gave me a perfunctory "Love you," as he hastily made his way over to the slide. As I tried to dispel my overly suspicious feeling, I recalled an observation Joe the psychologist often makes: Just because you're paranoid, doesn't mean they're not out to get you!

So why was Joe in such a rush to kiss me off? As Joe jumped down the slide, a blast of heat rushed through my body, while I instinctively scanned the boat for Justine. But surprise—Justine was nowhere to be found!

Nervously on edge, I took off for the side of the boat near the caves, and lo and behold, Justine was swimming away with Joe. I was fuming, but way too intoxicated to go after them. I would deal with Joe later.

Gwen was doing her usual routine—zipping about and desperately checking around for Danny while maniacally calling out his name. Meanwhile, I was doing my own checking around for Joe. As I danced with the twins, I was craning my neck backward every couple of seconds to keep on top of *The Joe and Justine Show*. As they frolicked in the water, Justine had the gall to wrap her arms around Joe's neck and rub her naked boobs all over his chest! As the jealousy oozed out of my body, I suddenly noticed Joe wince and yell up to the boat crew that he had stepped on something. While I wanted to feel bad that he was in pain, I was secretly elated to see that whatever had just happened got Justine and her boobies off Joe.

Payback is a bitch. The staff carried Joe onto the deck and examined the bottom of his feet. They explained that he had stepped on sea urchins and that the spines in his feet needed immediate removal. They pulled out their first aid kit and grabbed a pair of medical long nose nipper pliers. I tried not to show my satisfaction. The boat staffers further explained that sea urchin spines were painful but not lethal and that they were going to pull out as many as possible. "Not lethal?" Joe asked, alarmed. After what my snake of a husband had pulled in the water, I was hoping they were just a tiny bit lethal.

When Joe lifted his feet for the crewmen to examine, the bottoms were chock full of spines and a bloody mess. While everyone else gasped, I was concentrating on trying to fake concern.

Joe was still sporting scabby, scraped knees from his water-skiing misadventure of a few days before. Even though Joe appeared to be in sorry shape, I wasn't feeling much sympathy for him. I loved Joe, but he had some nerve sneaking behind my back with that floozy Justine. I found his being splayed flat on his back, writhing in pain, with his feet up in the air, flanked by a crew member on each foot, to be appropriate retribution.

Joe, suddenly remembering he had a wife, gazed at me forlornly. I responded with a peppy smile and a double "thumbs-up." Joe was rattled as they picked the spines out from his feet. No doubt, all thoughts of Justine and her jugs had by now escaped his mind. Suddenly he was happy to be back with the always reliable Julie.

But after his Justine spectacle, Joe was getting no pity points from me—especially when Celine pulled me aside and told me that Justine had been giving guys stiffies the whole day. "What's a stiffy?" I asked her.

She vigorously moved her index finger up and down. I shook my head in disbelief. *Thank you, sea urchins.*

When we got back to the dock, Stan and David helped Joe off the boat and back to our room. He was claiming to be in excruciating pain, so I decided to keep the what-goes-around-comes-around sermon to myself, and I stayed in the room with him until he fell asleep.

While Joe slept, I snuck out to the prude beach and was writing in my journal when Mary arrived. "We haven't had a chance to talk about the other night," she said modestly, glimpsing over my shoulder to see what I was writing.

"I know; I feel awkward about the whole incident and have been trying to avoid discussing it," I replied as I closed the journal as inconspicuously as possible.

"There is nothing to feel awkward about," Mary responded. "We were both so trashed, we barely have a clue what happened in that hammock anyway," she said, pointing to the "scene of the crime." As we studied the hammock, Mary blabbed on. "But what little I do remember still gives me the butterflies." She fluttered her hands up and down, while I lamely flapped along with her.

Then we climbed into the hammock and lay close together. As we swayed back and forth, I mustered up the courage to speak out. "If you want my honest opinion, awkward as it is to discuss, I think we had a memory-making moment the other night. But without a doubt, I still want to keep quiet about what happened between us, even though we barely remember what happened." I was rambling, but I kept right on going for fear that I would back out of the conversation altogether. "The thought occurred to me that we more than likely put a foot in the lady pond. Plus, life is short, and so that got me thinking that maybe you and Stan…"

Mary interrupted me. "Wait, you want to have a threesome with Stan and me?"

"Ew! NO. I thought we could have a foursome!" *There, I said it!*

The initial shock on Mary's face was enough to make me want to follow up with "just kidding," but then her face softened, and she gave me a bashful and oh-so-sweet smile.

"You know what, Julie? It *does* make sense. I mean, who would I rather hang out with? You and I obvi have a physical attraction, and I feel so comfortable around you—and Joe as well, for that matter." I gave Mary an affectionate embrace. *Obvi?*

"But it doesn't have to be anything more than what we want it to be, right?" I wasn't sure what Mary wanted it to be, nor was I sure what in the hoo-ha I wanted it to be, but I said, "Exactly."

"Then it's settled," she said, and we gave each other a loving hug.

"Yes—settled," I answered back at her, still hugging her tightly.

"Now let's go for a swim," she said flippantly.

Settled? We hadn't settled on much of anything but the bare basics of our planned encounter.

On our way to the pool, we saw Baryl and David. Baryl had a long welt across both legs. "Let me guess," I said drolly. "Olga was in the house."

Baryl was shamefaced but gamely replied, "Ah always was a suckah for a good lookin' gal."

David turned around to show me a red mark on his back. "Me too," he said sheepishly.

After swimming, we all decided to wake up Joe and

get ready for dinner. I could tell that Joe was still irritated by my reaction to his latest disaster, but after a few minutes, he was mostly back to his old self, although he was limping a bit. *Not even an ocean of poisonous sea urchins could deter Joe from the Exotica action.*

At the bar, before dinner, we were still checking people out, and Joe pointed out a physically fit couple, giving us the once-over. When they approached us, the guy introduced himself as Marcus and told Joe he was a gynecologist and that his girlfriend, Kirstin, was his assistant. As they turned their attention to the couple next to us, Joe asked, "What do you think?"

"We should never settle for anything less than a doctor," I answered sarcastically. We decided they weren't "the ones" when Marcus started to discuss vagina, clitori, and vulva disorders. Kirstin repeatedly called her vagina her Virginia. Way too much genital talk for me.

As the two of us stood at the bar alone, I brought up the idea of Mary and Stan. "The V Mary?" Joe asked, caught off guard. "The visual image of Mary crouched in the corner of Kendra and Don's bed, with her eyes glued shut, is not exactly a turn-on, Julie," he continued.

"She's the only one I think I can do this with, Joe," I pleaded as he elbowed me in the side. When I turned around, Mary and Stan were right behind me. "Speaking of the devils," I said lightheartedly.

While Sam and Joe were joking around, Mary mouthed to me that she had spoken to Stan. I was half hoping Stan had put the kibosh on the whole thing. She leaned in and said quietly, "I told Stan about your idea, and he's in."

Stan's in?! At that moment, it hit me that my big mouth and moronic idea had put me in a situation that I was not going to be able to get out of easily. *You made your bed, and now you're going to have to sleep in it. With freakin Stan!*

"We need a plan," Mary blurted out. "Let's strategize over drinks," I replied, while mentally strategizing a way out of my brilliant idea.

"Knowing the way we roll, we will need a stockpile of booze, so let's start now," Mary said as the two of us hurried to the bar for some Jell-O shots.

At dinner, we caroused with our new homies, and I thought about how much I was going to miss every one of them. Looking around, I was reminded of how ironic it was that, although we had ended up in Exotica because of a mistake, we had met so many people who just might be in our lives forever. We all exchanged phone numbers and email addresses and vowed to get together again soon.

"We're fixin' to go to Toga Tony's party in New York if y'all wanna join us," Baryl said, pumping her fists in the air.

"I'm not sure about that," I replied, "but perhaps we'll come to visit you in Kentucky." *Perhaps what??*

"Inytime, inywhere," replied Baryl in her southernly sugary voice. When she broke into a smile, it jolted me with an electric current. *Perhaps I should have kept my big mouth shut.* Baryl pursed her full lips and then slowly fluttered her long silky eyelashes as if to invite me in.

After dinner, a bunch of us noticed what seemed to be gym equipment, and a raised platform set up on the beach. As we got closer, I heard Mary gasp, "Shut the front door."

What now? I thought as I squinted to read the sign. "BDSM slave auction?" I asked apprehensively.

"Bondage, discipline, sadism, and masochism," Olga said with a twinkle in her eye.

"Excited!" I replied cynically as I gave Baryl an eye roll.

"Come on, shugah, let's give this slave auction a whirl," she said as she took me over to an unforgettable scene of weird-looking machinery set up around a stage. To the right of the stage was a jumbo tent full of air mattresses, with a sign that read "Dungeon Playroom." On each side of the tent stood a behemoth bald guy.

As I tiptoed closer to the tent, there was a woman dressed in a latex jumpsuit and a spiked leather collar with an attached chain-link leash, giving out "daddy bucks" to be used for the auction bidding. *Puh-leeze.* She handed me the "rules." I peeked into the tent and saw a middle-aged man in a diaper lashing a middle-aged woman with a cat-o'-nine-tails-type whip. I stuck my finger in my mouth like I was going to gag myself and fixed my gaze on Olga and Baryl.

"ABDL," said Olga.

"ABD what?" I asked, bemused.

"Adult baby diaper lover," replied Olga. This time when I stuck my finger in my mouth, I gave an aargh sound.

Even Baryl pitched in with, "Ahm gittin queasy, y'all."

"Whips, canes, and nipple clamps on request," I recited from the pamphlet the latex lady had given me, feeling queased out myself. "Oh, let me run my diaperless ass over there and request all three," I muttered under my breath. Joe and Stan hovered over me like eager beavers as I continued to read. "Choose top or bottom before proceeding to the slave tent for doubles delight. Do I dare ask what top or bottom means?" I scoured the group, waiting for someone to answer.

Gwen stared at me intently, and I assumed she was going to shed some light on the subject. But without fail, all she wanted to know was, "Have you seen Danny?"

Leave it to Olga, the mistress of black and blue, to perk up with the answer. "The top is dominant; the bottom is submissive," she said feverishly. "So, for example, the top ties the bottom up, which puts the bottom at the top's mercy, and then the top plays with the bottom, teasing, seducing, frustrating, and hopefully finally satisfying. I highly recommend you try it," she said in all seriousness.

Yeah, like I might. And then, as if I wasn't already sick enough of Joe's recent behavior, he tried to give me those eyes of his. "In your mcdreams," I said icily.

As I stomped away, I saw the mermaid dressed up in nothing but a fishing net, while the fisherman pointed his finger in her face, saying, "You've been a bad little fishy, and now I have to tie you up and spank you!"

While I grimaced, Olga hooked her arm through mine and dragged me back towards the stage. Men and women were furiously waving their daddy bucks in the air and loudly bidding on four leather-clad brunette she-slaves who were posing naked, and handcuffed. As the slaves were auctioned off one by one to the highest bidders, I eyed Olga, who was thoroughly enjoying herself. *Am I the only one turned off here?*

It was evident that the answer was *yes*, since a throng of onlookers, including my overly enthusiastic husband, were congregating around the stage, either observing the proceedings or actively participating in the bidding for the sex slaves!

"There is power in submitting to someone who wants to inflict pain on you; it's a fantastic gesture of trust," Olga said as she made suggestive eye contact.

Complete and utter bullshit, I thought to myself as I tried to ignore the frenetic bidders surrounding me.

"I'm here," announced Danny as he popped out of the shadows. "Follow me," he instructed Gwen, who was so elated to see him that she was prepared to do whatever necessary to keep him close by. As they hurried off to inquire about the "next steps," the rest of the crew trailed close behind. And me—what else? I was dragged along with the rest of them.

We arrived at a counter where a young woman with piercings in her ears, nose, eyebrows, and mouth was teaching beginner rope bondage methods and explaining how to play with needles and fire.

"On what planet do the words *needles* and *fire* go with

the word *play?*" I asked Miss Pierced Face. She looked at me with disdain. *She's looking at ME with disdain?*

"Where do we sign up?" asked an animated Danny while Gwen observed skeptically.

"You will need to speak to a DM," Pierced Face told Danny while staring me down.

"And what exactly is a DM?" I asked pleasantly, not giving one iota.

"A DM is a dungeon monitor," she curtly responded.

I gazed around in horror. "If Babe is involved, I'm out," I said emphatically. Like I was ever going to be in, Babe or no Babe.

As the Britney Spears song "I'm a Slave 4 U" was wafting in the background, Pierced Face said, "It's Babe's night off." She promptly summoned over a bald guy with a tattoo of a dragon on his head.

"Great news about Babe," said Joe, visibly relieved and clapping his hands together like an idiot, while Stan stood there bouncing his head up and down like a bobblehead until Mary flicked the side of his temple with her fingers.

"Choose your equipment," said the bald DM to Danny, who ran over to a mega wooden X with metal cuffs on each of its four ends and summoned Gwen. Gwen slowly walked over and looked back at us miserably. The

DM gave Danny a latex thong and a matching tank top and told him to put them on. *No real man should ever wear a thong in public*, I thought distastefully.

As we all looked on, stupefied, Danny stripped off his clothes and did as he was told. Then the DM attached him to the X, with his backside facing us and his hands and feet tethered to the four corners. He put a collar on Danny and pulled it snugly around his neck. "What's your safe word?" the DM asked. "Safe" would not be a word I would use to describe the scene I was witnessing.

"I don't need a safe word," Danny said confidently, looking over his shoulder at the DM.

"Your call," the DM said as he handed Gwen the whip. "If you don't comply with the rules, I will have to remove you both from the premises immediately. Otherwise, you're in good hands on my watch." Call me cynical, but I was not buying the "good hands" assurance. And immediately leaving the premises sounded like an okay idea to me.

We were all aghast when Gwen took the leather whip and proceeded to flog Danny's minimally clad butt. "Get your act together," Danny sniped meanly. At first, Gwen looked offended, then incensed, as she asked the DM for a gag. Over Danny's protests, Gwen shoved the gag into his mouth and tightly knotted it behind his head. As Gwen whipped Danny, he was barking at her, but with the gag, we had no idea what he was saying.

Clearly, this was going to be payback time for all those many occasions that Danny had wandered off to do his own thing, leaving Gwen no choice but to search for him non stop. Gwen was visibly annoyed at Danny, but clearly on a mission, and she seemed to be getting more aggressive as the whipping progressed.

After a few minutes, Danny was yelping like a wounded dog, and Gwen looked like she'd had enough. But she surprised all of us when she loudly proclaimed, "That's what you get for being a jerk and running off all the time without me. And now I finally get to give you the beating you deserve!" At that point, Gwen threw down the whip and stormed off, leaving Danny tethered to the X. Mary chased after Gwen while Danny gagged and bound, looked on pathetically. *Well, at least Gwen knows he's not going anywhere*, I thought.

Then the DM looked around and boomed out, "WE NEED A DOMINATRIX. CALLING FOR A DOMINATRIX!"

We all stared at each other in wonderment as an erotic statuesque blonde woman emerged from the masses. Joe instantly proclaimed her an "11." Like Moses parting the waters of the Red Sea, the crowd created a pathway in the sand for her. *Hopefully, Danny's journey will last less than forty years,* I reflected.

The dominatrix walked purposefully up to Danny on the X. Still unable to speak because of the gag, Danny gave the dominatrix a wink, and even with the gag in his mouth, not to mention his suddenly erect phallus, it was evidence that euphoria had replaced his seconds-before whimpering face. That was until she started to whip the shit out of him. As he mewled in pain, he tried to beseech the crowd, howling through his gag.

I wanted to say; *You're tethered spread-eagle to a gargantuan X. Did you think this was going to be a walk in the park?* But all I could do was to shout out to poor Danny boy, "I guess a safe word would have come in handy just about now," before I dashed off to locate Gwen and Mary.

I found them at the Group Therapy bar and told Gwen about Danny's happenstance. As Gwen scrambled to rescue Danny, I clenched Mary's hand, and we reluctantly walked back to the surreal scene.

Danny was off the X, rubbing his beet-red butt and admonishing Gwen. In turn, Gwen was loudly proclaiming to Danny that he had gotten what he deserved. *Go, Gwen, go, Gwen*, I sing-songed to myself.

Mary and I searched around for the guys, who were AWOL. We eventually located them at the dungeon, raptly watching a couple having sex, like two peeping toms. As we stormed over to Joe and Stan, we heard wailing and saw the girl seemingly fighting for her life, trying to get the guy off of her. I started to jump in for the save, but Joe pulled me back. "It's a rape fantasy," he said calmly.

"It's a *WHAT*?" I asked, startled.

"Kinky, huh?" he said in a barely audible whisper, like a real creepola.

"Not so much," I said, grabbing Joe's wrist and dragging him out of there like an errant child. Stan and Mary meekly followed.

As we were leaving, we bumped into Olga and Yuri. "I'd love to buy you a slave. How about it?" Olga asked me lustily, fanning out her daddy bucks. *How about backing off, bitch,* I thought as I ignored her question and bolted out of there.

The four of us made our way back to the bar. I was regretting my hookup idea and hoping that the V Mary would chicken out. While Mary and I stood to the side chatting, we observed Joe and Stan having a heart-to-heart. It looked as if our plan was about to be implemented. *But it's not too late to back out,* I unconvincingly assured myself.

Joe announced that we were all going back to our room for a drink. I took one look at Joe and knew that he and Stan had the "talk." Mary and I eyeballed each other, and the look of concern on both of our faces actually helped settle us down. We were both pitifully wasted and reassessing our earlier hookup decision.

On our way to the room, Joe was ahead of us with Stan, while Mary and I dawdled behind. *This is your last chance to get out of this mess*, I vehemently reminded myself. As I angled for a way out of my not-so-brilliant suggestion, Mary said she had it all figured out. I was relieved and was fairly certain she was going to say we should forget about the whole idiotic idea.

"I'll take Joe to my room, and you take Stan to yours; that way, neither one of us has to see anything upsetting." My heart sank. Mary was ready to do this—and without me in the room?! I didn't want to distress Mary by rejecting her suggestion, and although I desperately wanted to back out, I kept quiet about my apprehension and gave her a weak nod of approval.

Mary gave me a tight squeeze, nestled herself in between Stan and Joe, and briefly spoke to them as they both agreed in unison. Then Mary took Joe's arm, turned around nervously, and mouthed *good luck* before they made a sharp left toward her room. *What do I need to do to unjoin this team?*

When my attention eventually came back to Stan, he looked at my gloomy expression and put his hand on my shoulder. "If you want, we can forget about this whole thing, Julie," he said, miserably deflated.

Every party has a pooper; that's why we invited you, I sang to myself as Stan stared at me quizzically. As I struggled to find something to say to Stan, we continued the journey to my room in silence. The whole time, I was moving as slowly as possible, sweating so profusely that the back of my hair was soaking wet. I started fanning myself, as Stan studied me. "Hot flash," was all I could muster up the courage to say as I continued to trudge to my room like I was going to a gauntlet. There was nothing remotely hot or flashy about the scenario. *What can I say to get out of this?*

I ticked off some ideas. *I have a yeast infection. My doctor said I shouldn't have sex until I have the lumps in my vaginal canal removed. I respect you too much. I'm still recovering from gender reassignment surgery.*

When we got to my room, Stan suggested we get into the hot tub and began to take off his clothes. I snuck into the bathroom and came out in my bathing suit, while Stan was naked and rarin' to go.

I slowly got into the water, and Stan put his hands around my waist. *Goddamn it; Stan has a stiffy*, I thought as I tried not to lose my cool. He gently kissed me on my forehead, my cheek, and my neck, but when he got to my lips, I started to wince. "I'm so sorry, Stan. Give me a minute."

"Let's have a drink," he dejectedly suggested, so we wrapped ourselves in towels and raided the mini-bar. As we drank straight out of the airline-sized vodka bottles, I stuffed my mouth with peanuts. I wasn't sure if I had one stuck in my throat, or I was hyperventilating, but either way, I couldn't breathe. When I went into a coughing and choking fit, Stan asked me if I needed the Heimlich. I shook my head *no*, thinking that what I needed was a savage beating for coming up with the asinine idea in the first place. *The S&M dungeon would have been better than this!*

Stan was anxious and uncomfortable about my complete meltdown and didn't know what to say or do about the current state of affairs. "Julie, listen, we're not in a rush. Let's relax for a few minutes and take it slow." He got a couple more mini vodkas, and we sat on the edge of the bed, guzzling in deafening silence.

"Sorry," I finally said weakly. Then I said sorry again.

And again. And again.

"Please don't apologize," he kept replying.

I was genuinely feeling regret about my freak out. Stan was terrific, and an undeniably handsome guy. It was so wrong of me to make him feel rejected and uncomfortable, particularly after it had been my short-sighted idea in the first place.

Yet I couldn't shake off my serious unease. For more years than I dared to count, I had been exclusive with Joe, and it was unrealistic to think that I could hook up with another man.

We went back and forth with "sorry" and "please don't apologize" so many times that we finally just cracked up at the absurdity of it all.

Then Stan leaned over and patted me on my head. *A head pat?* How humiliating! I had majorly loused up our night.

I put my head in Stan's lap as he reassured me that he was genuinely okay with us not doing anything, even though I still felt his stiffy through the towel. We both decided that it was too much too soon. Well, I decided that it was too much too soon, and Stan suggested we kill some time at the beach and enjoy the full moon.

I was heartsick imagining what Mary and Joe were up

to, fairly sure she wasn't dry heaving on peanuts. As we inched our way to the beach, I tried to keep all thoughts of Joe and Mary out of my head. I finally couldn't take it anymore and confessed to Stan about my fear of not being able to be friends with them once Joe and Mary hooked up. We both promised to suck it up, accept whatever the consequences would be, and remain friends.

While I fought back tears, Stan was unsuccessfully trying to cheer me up. I was overwhelmed and mentally preparing myself for what was sure to be a painful reunion with Mary and Joe.

When we reached the ocean, I saw a couple sitting and leaning on each other near the water's edge. The closer we got, the better I was able to see, and all of a sudden, I heard, "Julie, is that you?"

Thank you, God! It was Joe's voice! Like in a movie, I ran to him, and Mary ran to Stan, and we threw our arms around each other, twirling and spinning. I jumped on Joe, who winced in pain from his sea-urchin-impaled feet, and we both comically tumbled into a heap on the sand.

"Did you…?" Joe started to ask, and I shook my head an emphatic *no*.

Mary glanced over at Stan and said, "You didn't do anything? Oh my God, neither did we!" Then the four of us hugged each other so hard that we all fell intertwined in the sand. We were wheezing and yowling and trying to catch our breath.

I planted a massive kiss on Mary's lips and let out a "whew." Then I repeated it over and over: whew, whew, whew, with Mary chiming in with me. The guys eye-balled each other, perplexed. I was clinging onto Mary, proclaiming, "Holy shit, nothing happened. Thank you, thank you, thank you." A few couples drifted by and were gawking at us rolling around in the sand, hoping to get a glimpse of wild sex between the four of us. The attention we were getting from passersby started us roaring again, and we were writhing around, holding our sides since they hurt so much.

Mary and I were past exhausted, both physically *and* mentally, from the night's events, so we all gave each other one final victory huddle and weaved back to our rooms. So much for the hookup.

When we reached our room, instead of our usual great sex, we had a great talk, and I have to say, it was almost (I said almost) as good as the sex we had been having. We didn't fall asleep until the sun was coming up, and it was the most romantic last night to what had turned out to be a weirdly fantastic vacation.

DAY 7

THE SOUND OF POUNDING AT OUR DOOR WOKE US out of our deep sleep. I glanced at the clock, and it was almost noon, which meant we had to leave for the airport in less than three hours. "We brought y'all breakfast," Baryl announced as she barged in with a tray of food and an entourage of people. The whole gang was squeezed into our room as I rubbed the sleep and mascara out of my eyes. "Ah hate goodbahs, so yer not gittin one from me," drawled Baryl.

Mary took my face in her hands and stuck her lower lip out dismally. "I'm going to miss you so much," she said tearfully.

As my eyes welled up, Sam said, "You're also going to miss the hot tub at four, but eat fast, and we can squeeze in some tub action before you leave." Leave it to Sam to ruin the tender moment.

The hot tub was jam-packed with the big women who love big men, hands in the air dancing, and calling my name. "After you," I said to Sam.

"The last one in is a rotten egg," he said as he jumped in. The rest of us decided that there were worst things than being rotten eggs. Way worse. So, we left Sam to his own devices while he pleaded for us to come back.

The bunch of us spent the next two hours basking on the beach, drinking champagne, and rehashing our vacation rowdiness. When Gwen and Danny showed up, Celine couldn't stop apologizing to them. "We had a snafu last night," Celine whispered in my ear.

YOU had a snafu last night? Get in line, I thought as I asked her what happened.

"We hooked up with Gwen and Danny," she responded.

"So, his penis is back in business?" I asked her playfully.

"I guess," she said with a shrug. "Danny finally got up the courage to have sex with me, but I was so tired that by the time the two of us got rolling, I fell asleep."

"Are you telling me that you fell asleep while having sex with the poor guy?" I asked, astounded.

"Hey, at least I didn't break anything this time," she

answered sheepishly.

Falling asleep having sex, and with somebody else's husband, no less? No, no, and no. But I did have to admit that I felt closer to Celine and the others than I had ever been to any of our friends back home. Although, I could have passed on all the gory sex details.

As Joe and I rolled our suitcases out to the lush lobby, a bunch of our new chums stopped by to see us off. We all hugged and exchanged more phone numbers, emails and promises to keep in touch. As absurd as it sounds, it was tough leaving them behind—but Mary was the toughest of them all. When I glanced at her, she was tearful and visibly upset, and we gave each other a loving embrace. She promised to call me when she got back home the following day.

As the bus pulled away, everyone was waving goodbye to us, and I was unprepared for how genuinely sad I was about leaving. I peered through the back window, waving goodbye to Giselle, Justine, Danny, and the rest of our newfound, stark naked friends until I couldn't see them any longer.

As we stood in line at the airport check-in, Joe and I reminisced about our trip. We prattled on about how much fun we'd had and what an eye-opening experience it had been. We recollected and wisecracked about each wild, weird, and insane Exotica scene—one after another, verbally and visually rewinding the events of the vacation playfully.

When we got to the counter, the customer service agent typed in our flight information and informed us that there was a snowstorm in New York. "We canceled hundreds of flights yesterday and today, and we're canceling all future flights for at least two days," she explained. "But don't worry; we will get you right back to your hotel, where you can stay for the next day or so, at the airline's expense."

I stared at the ticket agent, mouth agape. *You have got to be kidding me.* I didn't know if I should be horrified at not being able to get back to our kids, our family, and our jobs, or elated that our astonishing and mind-altering expedition was about to be extended!

But on second thought, the answer was eminently clear. We needed to get back to New York. We needed to see our kids. We needed to get back to work. *If you can hear me, God, we really need to get back to our normal, sober, boring life. Yes, please give me my normal and boring back.*

Then I turned to Joe, who was wearing the widest of grins on his face—and, of course, that by-now-familiar and most annoying twinkle in his stupid baby blues.

ABOUT THE AUTHOR

TERI SCHURE IS THE FOUNDER OF THE international news website Worldpress.org, a journalist, writer, blogger, and publishing and marketing consultant.

Her blog *The Teri Tome* attracts over 30,000 page views per month, plus an additional 50,000 on her website Worldpress.org.

Ms. Schure has been a director at Newsweek, a publisher, and COO of *World Press Review* magazine, and in 1997 was *Commentary* magazine's first female publisher since their founding in 1945.

She enjoys a successful freelance career in newspaper and magazine publishing, freelance writing, and government event planning.

Contact her, or visit her web site at TeriSchure.com or read her blog at blog.terischure.com.